The Fates Will Find Their Way

Hannah Pittard

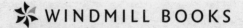WINDMILL BOOKS

Published by Windmill Books 2012

2 4 6 8 10 9 7 5 3 1

Copyright © Hannah Pittard 2011

First published in Great Britain in 2011 by William Heinemann

Windmill Books
The Random House Group Limited
20 Vauxhall Bridge Road, London SW1V 2SA

Addresses for companies within The Random House Group Limited can be found at:
www.randomhouse.co.uk/offices.htm

The Random House Group Limited Reg. No. 954009

www.randomhouse.co.uk

A CIP catalogue record for this book
is available from the British Library

ISBN 9780099537748

The Random House Group Limited supports The Forest Stewardship Council
(FSC®), the leading international forest certification organisation. Our books
carrying the FSC label are printed on FSC® certified paper. FSC is the only forest
certification scheme endorsed by the leading environmental organisations,
including Greenpeace. Our paper procurement policy can be found at:
www.randomhouse.co.uk/environment

Printed and bound by CPI Group (UK) Ltd, Croydon, CR0 4YY

Hannah Pittard's fiction has appeared in *McSweeney's*, the *Oxford American*, the *Mississippi Review*, BOMB, Nimrod, and *StoryQuarterly*, and was included in 2008 *Best American Short Stories' 100 Distinguished Stories*. She is the recipient of the 2006 Amanda Davis Highwire Fiction Award and a graduate of the University of Virginia's MFA program. She divides her time between Charlottesville and Chicago, where she currently teaches fiction at DePaul University.

Praise for *The Fates Will Find Their Way*

'Blurs the boundaries between memory, imagination, fantasy and delusion . . . It's a startling piece of work . . . Pittard powerfully evokes the intense contradictions of adolescence: the capacity to feel dread, boldness, vulnerability, nostalgia and desire in a single instant . . . It is an unflinching account of the dark undercurrents of youthful sexuality; of the messy, often brutal reality of our instincts; and of the dreamlike coating that time applies to our memories.'

Observer

'It's hard not to think of *The Virgin Suicides* when reading this novel . . . The tone is wistful, lustful, gossipy, guilty – everything that made *The Virgin Suicides* such a remarkable debut when it came out in 1993. But it would be unfair to call Pittard's book derivative. Where *The Virgin Suicides* had a good old gothic wallow in its adolescent turmoil, *The Fates Will Find Their Way* is more meditative . . . It's a coming-of-age story in which everyone is all ages, all the time . . . She does a beautifully delicate job . . . There is a buzz about Pittard in the US, where her short stories have appeared in literary journals such as *McSweeney's*, BOMB and *Story Quarterly* . . . She's undoubted'' ''''''' '' '''''' '' '''''''''''' '''''''''' debut about a lost girl

Guardian

'When a publisher likens a debut novel to a previous blockbuster, it often feels like wishful thinking. Not so in this instance. Hannah Pittard's tender, savvy tale of murky goings-on in suburban basements is forcibly reminiscent of Jeffrey Eugenides's hit *The Virgin Suicides* . . . Like Eugenides's book before it, this deeply readable novel concerns itself with mysteries that are at once more mundane and more profound – innocence, longing, the winding journey to adulthood.'

Daily Mail

'A haunting debut with echoes of *The Virgin Suicides* . . . turn dreamy, regretful and melancholy, the velvety prose explores "what if" territory, offering alternative endings for the missing girl.'

Marie Claire

'Dreamlike . . . Unusual and compelling.'

Grazia

'Impressive . . . A story about the dark matter of adolescent desire that pulls on the heart across decades . . . A Poignant testimony of male adolescence, steeped in nostalgia and regret . . . Chilling and touching. Pittard can be harrowingly wise about the melancholy process of growing up.'

Washington Post

'One of the most impressive aspects of *The Fates Will Find Their Way* is how it summons up the elements of a suburban youth . . . Deeply felt . . . At its core it's about how children become adults.'

New York Times Book Review

For Malcolm Hugh Ringel,
who disappeared from our lives June 16, 2006

What each man does will shape his trial and fortune.
For Jupiter is king to all alike; the fates will find their way.

—Virgil, *The Aeneid*

THE FATES WILL FIND
THEIR WAY

Some things were certain; they were undeniable, inarguable. Nora Lindell was gone, for one thing. There was no doubt about that. For another, it was Halloween when she went missing, which only served to compound the eeriness, the mysteriousness of her disappearance. Of course, it wasn't until the first day of November that most of us found out she was gone, because it wasn't until the day after Halloween that her father realized she hadn't come home the night before and so started calling our parents.

From what we could tell, and from how the phone tree was ordered that year, Jack Boyd's parents got the first phone call. Mrs. Boyd, as prescribed by the tree, called Mrs. Epstein, who called Mrs. Zblowski, who called Mrs. Jeffreys. By the time the tree had been completed, many mothers had already gotten word of Nora's disappearance either from us–running from house to house–or from Mr. Lindell himself, who'd broken phone-tree etiquette and continued making calls even after getting off the phone with Mrs. Boyd. It was a breach in etiquette that our mothers forgave, obviously, but one that they agreed tacitly, behind the back of Mr. Lindell, added unnecessarily to the general confusion of the day.

The phone tree produced no new information. But it did, accidentally, serve to remind our mothers that the time change had come late that year and that all the clocks should be set back an hour. How we'd forgotten, none of us knew. But somewhere in the branches and twigs of the phone tree, a mother remembered that in addition to having lost Nora, we'd gained an hour. All our mothers could do was promise Mr. Lindell to ask us about his daughter when we returned home that night, an hour later than they expected.

With our curfew the same but with the day that much longer, while our mothers waited at home for our return, while the leaves changed and fell seemingly in a single afternoon, turned from green to orange to pewter to nothing, we stayed outdoors and away from our parents. We stayed away from the girls as best we could—all but Sarah Jeffreys who, for various reasons, was nearly impossible to want to stay away from—as though allegiance to our own sex would somehow solve the mystery, once we'd learned of it, all the faster. We interrogated each other for information, eager to be the one to discover the truth. As it turned out, we'd all seen Nora the day before, but seen her in different places doing different things—we'd seen her at the swing sets, at the riverbank, in the shopping mall. We'd seen her making phone calls in the telephone booth outside the liquor store, inside the train station, behind the dollar store. We'd seen her in her field hockey sweats, in her jean jacket, in her uniform. We saw her smoking a cigarette, sucking a lollipop, eating a hot dog. Surely she'd gone to the midnight thriller trilogy with us all (we called it the midnight show, though it was over by ten, just in time for curfew), and yet when we questioned each other—asked who had gotten to sit next to her, to share popcorn with her, to scare her when she was least expecting it—none of us could take credit.

Trey Stephens, the only public schooler among us, was the last to find out since his parents weren't on the tree. He lived in the neighborhood and we'd known him forever. His was the largest basement, with neon beer signs and stolen street signs, a giant fish tank and two dartboards, a full-size pool table and a drum kit.

shaved her legs in front of him. Though this seemed even more unlikely than the sex—doubtful they'd be in a basement by themselves, let alone a bathroom—we closed our eyes at the beauty of the notion, at the very possibility of the idea. We closed our eyes and saw what Trey Stephens had seen. Some of us imagined her sitting in the bathtub. Others saw her standing, first her left leg propped up on the shower ledge and then her right. We begged Trey for more details, though deep down we knew that too many specifics would shatter the images we'd formed so delicately in our minds.

Drew Price—who insisted almost daily and somewhat frantically that he would one day be as tall as his father, which suggested he didn't know or didn't believe what the rest of us knew and believed, that Mr. Price wasn't his real father—said he'd seen Nora at the bus station on the day of Halloween. Winston Rutherford also said this, but he said she got into the passenger side of a beat-up Catalina just before the bus pulled out. The meeting place was a distraction, he said, meant to throw off possible witnesses like Drew Price. "Don't feel bad," Winston told Drew. "That's what anybody would have thought. It's just I kept looking. I saw what really happened." The driver of the Catalina was a man, but beyond that Winston's description of both man and car changed constantly.

Sometimes the Catalina had a broken taillight. Sometimes the rear window had a bullet hole. Sometimes the driver had a ponytail. Sometimes he had a mustache like a sailor. Always he smoked a cigarette.

As our curfew drew nearer, the stories became more lurid, more adult, more sinister, and somehow more believable. Sarah Jeffreys–who'd abandoned the girls that night in favor of our company, perhaps for the protection of boys and would-be men, though perhaps merely to avoid the clingy sadness of the girls, their willowy voices, their insistence that *It could have been me!*–said she drove Nora Lindell to the abortion clinic in Forest Hollow the day before Halloween, which seemed to lend credence to Trey Stephens' claim that he'd had sex with her the month before. Sarah had been sworn to secrecy, which is why she said she would never tell Nora's father. She–Nora– had taken the pregnancy test at school, while Sarah waited one stall over. Sarah said someone had left the window open in the girls' bathroom in the gymnasium and that Nora had complained that it was too cold to pee. Details like this we found convincing. A detail we didn't find convincing was that we'd never seen Sarah and Nora together before. We pointed this out. "Anyway," said Sarah. "Three hours after I dropped Nora off, I picked her up. She was standing right where I'd left her. We drove back to town together."

At ten p.m., half-spooked and more tired than we were willing to admit, relieved possibly that the curfew was finally upon us, we left Trey Stephens' house through the sliding glass doors in the basement. We left the public schooler alone, in his sad blue-carpeted basement with a pool cue in his hand, and we ran to our own homes maybe two doors, five doors, six blocks away. Shivering, we ran through the night, through the leaves and the cold, shouting our good nights to each other, not bothering to stop until we were safely through our front doors.

STRANGELY, IN THE MONTHS to come, it was Nora's younger sister, Sissy, who garnered much of our attention. We thought about Nora, of course. We wondered where she was, what she was doing. We told stories. But, the more time that passed and the more we began to understand she was really gone, the more we kept those fantasies to ourselves, saved them for the times we spent alone after school, in our bedrooms, or in the kitchen in the dark before anybody else was awake, when our stomachs ached from an emptiness both primitive and prehistoric.

With each other, we talked about Sissy Lindell, wondered what life must be like for her in that three-story Tudor at the foot of the cul-de-sac. Sissy, after all, was still among us. Still living, still real. Our fan-

tasies about her were therefore safer, easier. Paul
Epstein was the first one to notice how quickly she'd
changed; how she'd gone, in one summer, from
a middle schooler, a classic little sister, a complete
annoyance, to a full-blown nymph, a dewy-mouthed
ninth-grader whose mere promenade down a hallway
drove varsity captains wild with boyish lust.

We felt bad for her father, especially the summer
after Nora went missing, when we all noticed the
change in Sissy. We felt bad when the two of them
would walk down the sidewalks, still holding hands,
which we all thought was a little weird. We felt bad
because we couldn't help watching her walk, the
way her uniform skirt moved up and down, back
and forth against her thighs. We knew from the
uneven hem that she was one of those girls who
rolled the waists of their skirts to shorten the length,
which meant of course that she wanted us to look.
We felt bad that Mr. Lindell had to have a daughter and that we had to exist to see her. We felt bad
for aching to hold her hand, brush against her arm,
for having thought not only about that other daughter then but also this daughter now, and about how
she might shave her legs—sitting down or standing
up or maybe not at all. How had she even learned
without Nora or her long-dead mother there to show
her? But we felt bad mostly that Mr. Lindell didn't

still have two daughters for us to look at the way we looked at Sissy.

THERE'D GONE AROUND TOWN the suggestion that Halloween be skipped the following year—out of respect for the Lindells, of course, but also as a precaution for the other girls in our town. What if Nora really had been taken by a predator? What if the predator aimed to strike again? It was our parents who came up with the idea to do away with Halloween, but Paul Epstein—obsessed now with Sissy, convinced in fact of his love for her, his ability alone to see her sadness, her loneliness—persuaded Mrs. Epstein, who persuaded our mothers, even Sarah Jeffreys' mother, who, it turns out, was the origin of the suggestion that the holiday be cancelled, that Sissy would feel too much guilt if we didn't celebrate Halloween. She'd feel responsible, and how awful and unfair to add that to the poor girl's worries.

Mrs. Jeffreys acquiesced on the condition that she be in control of Halloween, that its celebration take place only in her basement and not on the streets. Our parents all agreed, relieved, and even little Sissy Lindell—red-haired, pink-lipped, mole-covered Sissy—attended. No doubt Paul Epstein regretted his determination to observe Halloween, because his heart was broken the night of the party when the rumor finally made its slow way to his position at the foosball table that Chuck Goodhue had walked into the mudroom off the Jeffreys' garage and seen Sissy Lindell with her face in the pants of Kevin Thorpe, a senior and starting center on the basketball team.

Mrs. Jeffreys, who wouldn't let Sarah use tampons because it was too much like having sex, walked into the mudroom not too long after Chuck Goodhue. And there, in one high-pitched breath, she purportedly ordered Kevin Thorpe to zip his fly and be ashamed of himself. Sissy she escorted home, holding her hand the entire way. She led her through the center of the party—Sissy blushing and with her head down but also undeniably smiling—all the way to the three-story Tudor, where she knocked on the door and handed Sissy over to Mr. Lindell. Whether or not she ratted out Sissy, none of us knew, but a handful of us did overhear Mrs. Jeffreys a few weeks later when she told Mrs. Epstein that she'd walked in on Kevin Thorpe saying, repeatedly, "Sit on it. Just sit on it."

"Can you imagine?" Mrs. Jeffreys said to Mrs. Epstein. "Can you even imagine?"

WE'D KNOWN SINCE NINTH grade that Sarah Jeffreys had been raped by Franco Bowles, Tommy Bowles' older brother, when he was home from college one summer. But it wasn't until years later—fully, if somewhat fitfully, situated in adulthood—that we were able to use this information to explain Mrs. Jeffreys' behavior. Too late we realized that what we'd always assumed was a nagging overprotectiveness was in fact a compulsive, if not remorseful, form of devotion to us all. We never forgave Franco for what he did. We never addressed it, but we never forgave him, either. And we all felt bad for not feeling bad sooner for Sarah. No one heard from Sarah after high school. She went missing too, in a way, but a different kind of missing.

Trey developed something of a fetish for girls in uniform. It wasn't his fault. We saw them every day. We got sick of the uniforms, hated the matching plaid skirts and the knee-high socks. We grew out of thinking they were sexy. But he was a public schooler; he never got the chance. A couple decades later, he went to jail after taking Paul Epstein's daughter home and doing things with her that girls shouldn't do until they're much, much older, if ever. Paul's daughter said she knew what she was doing. She said she wanted to do those things with Trey. But what does a thirteen-year-old know of what she wants? In the court testimony, she referred to Trey as Mr. Stephens. Never had we felt so old. She called Mr. Stephens a man; our sons she referred to as boys. We blushed at the wording. How simple, how true.

FOR TWO YEARS, MRS. Jeffreys controlled Halloween. If Sissy was invited to Sarah's basement party that second year, none of us knew about it and she certainly didn't attend. Plans had been made by Mr. Lindell to send his youngest away for her last two years of high school. She needed a fresh start, he said, needed not always to be thought of as Nora Lindell's little sister. Probably this was true. But mostly we blamed Paul Epstein, who'd taken to calling Sissy a slut in the hallways at school. She'd walk by, alone or with a girlfriend, and he'd cough the word into his hand from where he leaned against his locker. None of us joined him, and Sissy never acknowledged him. But always her face turned a horrible blotchy red, which was proof enough that she heard him every time.

Paul argued that you couldn't force someone into becoming something they weren't already, but mostly we agreed that Paul had pushed her into it. That, believing she already had the reputation, Sissy Lindell thrust herself into fulfilling what only Paul Epstein had alleged. At one point it was rumored that she'd even had sex with Trey Stephens. When we took it to him, however, he denied it. "I might go to public school," he said, "but I wouldn't do that to Nora." We couldn't help but respect his loyalty;

couldn't help but believe that he alone would have the dignity and self-restraint that the rest of us lacked. Of course, this was before Paul Epstein had a daughter, before any of us could even conceive of having daughters of our own.

By the time Sissy left for boarding school, bound for one of those inscrutable states in New England, we'd stopped speculating publicly about the whereabouts of Nora Lindell. It was impolite, for one thing. For another, it was just plain weird to indulge the interest; unhealthy to continue the conjectures. It appeared that our mothers, as we prepared to leave them, were finally rubbing off on us. We'd grown out of Halloween. Our complexions had evened out; our skin maintained a perfect equilibrium. We learned discretion from girls, about girls. We packed our trunks and suitcases, prepared for our natural and necessary moves away from home. Outwardly, we breathed sighs of relief at the somber comfort of growing up. Inwardly, we held our breath and tried to stand as still as possible, afraid we might be the only ones who didn't yet feel the promised calm of adulthood.

But it would be a lie to pretend that every one of us—alone finally, that last night of childhood, that last night before leaving for college—didn't close our eyes, perhaps in unison even, and imagine Nora Lindell. We closed our eyes, and we imagined both Nora and ourselves, ten years, twenty years from now. We imagined houses and cars and maybe even children. We imagined her there with us, more beautiful than our wives, more aloof, more tender, more kind. We imagined her future and our own. We closed our eyes and fell asleep to Nora Lindell, alive and happy. In the morning we advanced to adulthood, relieved at last of childhood fantasies.

But what if Drew Price and Winston Rutherford weren't lying? What if there really was a Catalina, and what if she really did get in? What if she didn't know the man but she'd seen him before, and when he leaned across and opened the passenger-side door, she got in? What if it was that simple?

They drove away together. It was an adventure, perhaps. But the experience that Nora had no doubt hoped would be intriguing turned quickly into something more menacing than mysterious. Almost immediately after she got in, she probably wanted to get out. It's the stuff of fantasies, not of real life. In fantasies, you can get into strangers' cars. You can have sex with men you don't know. They'll love you and pet you and whisper things that high school boys don't know to whisper. They'll fall hard for you and do anything you tell them to, including take you home whenever you want.

But the man in the Catalina didn't take Nora Lindell home. She waited too long to admit to herself she was in danger. She waited, unbelievably, out of politeness. It was dark by five o'clock, and it was the darkness that brought out the fear, but by then they were already far enough from Nora's town that she didn't know where they were. They were in the woods was all she knew. She felt strongly there was water nearby. She didn't look at him as they drove. She didn't talk to him, either, afraid that talking would give him the opportunity to confirm what she already knew. That this was it. That she was never going home.

The radio lost reception and the woods got thicker and the man turned the stereo off so that the little light that had been coming from its face was now gone. There were no stars, no moon. At least not that she could see through the tree cover. Perhaps it would snow. She turned her head towards the window and closed her eyes. She wanted the night to be over.

The car slowed. She felt his hand on her knee. She was still in her uniform and she regretted that. She wished she were wearing jeans, pants, something hard to pull off. She moved her knee away from his hand without looking at him. She pulled herself inward, upward, so that she was pressed fully against the passenger-side door. She did not open her eyes. The car stopped but he didn't turn off the ignition.

"You're cold," he said.

She didn't say anything.

"I can turn the heat up," he said.

She wanted to make herself invisible.

"But you have to ask me," he said.

She clenched shut her eyes until there was a throbbing, until the black behind her eyelids shot stars into her brain. She wanted to be at home again. She wanted to be trick-or-treating with Sissy and all of Sissy's idiot friends. She wanted to be a baby again, to be anything other than a girl. She wanted for sex not to exist. She wanted for Trey Stephens not to exist. She wanted for the aqua-blue aquarium and that basement and those boys to never have existed in the first place. She regretted her uniform. She regretted her legs and the urge ever to have shown off her knees. She regretted skin. Yes, skin. That was it. More than anything she regretted the existence of skin—hers or anyone else's.

"Hey," he said. His voice was young. Not young like hers, but smooth and easy like maybe he preferred singing to speaking. "Hey," he said again. He poked her in the side, and she opened her eyes. They were in the woods. There was no light, no house, no road.

"Why'd you get into my car?"

She tucked her legs under her body, pulled her skirt down so it covered her knees.

"I don't know," she said. She was crying.

"What if I told you I'd take you anywhere you wanted to go? What if I told you that?"

"Will you?" she said, looking at him finally. He was smiling. He was handsome even. She felt sick.

"That's not the question," he said. He reached towards her and she flinched, but he only opened the glove compartment and pulled out a box of cigarettes. "You smoke," he said.

"No," she said.

"Don't be a liar," he said. "Take one."

She took one. He struck a match and held it only partly towards her. She didn't lean forward, and he let the flame burn to his fingers.

"Are you being fussy with me?"

She shook her head.

"Seems like it though, doesn't it." He lit another match. "Doesn't it?"

"I'm sorry," she said.

"I know," he said. He lit his own cigarette, then held the match towards her, again only so far. "It's not going to light itself," he said.

Nora leaned forward, looking at the cigarette in her hand, at the murmur of flame in the middle of the car. She was aware of her mouth, of the heat on her cheeks, of his incredibly steady hand. She was conscious of these things, which meant he also was conscious of them. She inhaled as the tip of the cigarette closed in on the light. Their fingers touched. She moved immediately back to her corner. She was shaking from the cold.

"The question is this," he said. He used his hands when he talked. He moved them up and down as if he were giving a lecture, but as if the movements were inconsequential to the meaning. "If I told you I'd take you anywhere, what would you say? Where would you go?"

"Home," she said.

"You're lying again," he said. He rolled down his window a crack and blew the smoke up and out. "You like my car?" he said. He held the cigarette up, towards the crack, but he looked at Nora. "I know you like my car. That's why you got in it."

She tried to smile, but she couldn't. She was physically incapable of moving the muscles in her face. Her cheeks were wet and she wanted to wipe them but her hands weren't receiving commands. They weighed too much, more than they'd ever weighed before.

"You got ash on your skirt," he said. She looked down. Half the cigarette had landed in a heap on her lap. "You want me to wipe that off for you?"

She shook her head.

"No," he said. He smiled. "No, I didn't think so."

She looked around the car. There was an over-whelming sense of tidiness. Everything was white. The seats were white. The dash was white. She looked behind her. She couldn't see the floorboards in the back, but she guessed they were as tidy as the ones up front. There was a folded blanket on the backseat. She felt sick again. Her shoulders slumped. Her mus-cles were giving out one by one.

"Hey," he said. She held up her head, tried to focus on his words. "Where are you going to put that ash? You're not going to wipe it onto my floor, are you?"

She shook her head.

"No," he said. Again he smiled. "I didn't think so."

SHE TRIED THE PASSENGER door, but it was locked. She looked at him.

"You got to unlock it first," he said.

She nodded and did as she was told. The door opened easily and a gust of wind held it that way. She looked again at the man, realizing now that she was looking for permission, understanding finally that he was in control. The easier she made it for him, the easier he would make it for her. Maybe.

"Go on," he said, still with that smile, as if he were embarrassed to know more than she did. As if he were embarrassed to have to explain.

She inched backwards out the door, careful to keep the ash on her skirt, careful not to let any fall onto the interior. When she was outside, she stood up straight. The hem of her skirt raised up in the wind, and she quickly moved her hands to hold down the fabric against her thighs.

"Shut the door," he said. "It's cold in here."

She shut the door with her hip, not sure what else she was supposed to do.

The night was black, crowded with black. And the trees, though the leaves were beneath her feet now and not on the branches, felt somehow thick with overgrowth. Animal noises might have comforted her, or the noise of the water she believed was close by. But there was nothing but the wind and the sound of the engine.

She turned away from the car and closed her eyes. She could smell the cigarette smoke still coming from the crack in the driver's window. The car idled behind her and she realized now that she could also smell gasoline, an exhaust leak maybe, something that a boy could have identified more easily than she.

There was a knock on the glass behind her. She turned. The man's face loomed large in the passenger window, though his body hadn't left the driver's seat. He showed his teeth when he smiled.

"Hey," he said. His voice was muffled behind the glass, like he was speaking underwater. Like they were both underwater. She thought about laughing. "I've got an idea," he said. She waited; her fingers had lost feeling. She couldn't have opened the door and gotten back in if she'd wanted to. He rolled down the passenger window slightly.

"Take a walk," he said. Now his voice was clear, re-announcing the reality of the night.

She shook her head. "I don't understand." The words came out though her chin didn't move.

"You take a walk." He was nodding his head. He was excited by something. He giggled. "You take a walk and see what you think. Then you come back here and tell me what you want."

Nora pulled the sleeves of her shirt over her fingers. She crossed her arms and shoved her hands into her armpits. Her skirt moved in the wind. She looked at the woods around her, at the trees above her. She looked at the man, his enormous grin. "What if I don't come back?" she said finally.

He giggled again. "What if I'm not here?" he said.

She felt drunk, foggy. She wondered if her eyes were working properly.

"Be good out there," he said, more excited now, his giggle high-pitched and tinny. "Don't get lost, now."

AT FIRST SHE WALKED. A cliché maybe, but her heart felt like a fist that had worked itself into her throat. Every few paces, she turned and looked at the Catalina where it idled. She wondered at what point he would get out of the car, at what point would he pull the blanket from the backseat and follow her into the woods. She wondered if she was still close enough to hear the driver's-side door when and if he opened it.

She tried walking backwards, squinting to focus through the cold, afraid to lose sight of the car and its contents. The exhaust was milky and pink in the brake lights. The headlights gave out a glow maybe twenty, thirty feet in front of the car, illuminating a triangle of dead leaves that faded completely at the root of a large elm. The smaller the car got, the faster she moved. At one point, she stumbled over a tree stump and when she looked again in the direction from which she'd come, she couldn't see the Catalina, and that's when she ran. She ran for a long time, her breath and the leaves crunching under her feet the only sounds. Five minutes, twenty, she couldn't be certain. Her hands were numb, but she could feel the tears from the branches and brambles. She could feel the wetness of blood on her skin.

She started coughing when she saw the gap in the tree cover. There, above her, floated the moon that she'd forgotten existed. Such audacity that it would float so calmly, so smoothly. She coughed, and the sound scared her. Of course she'd made noise running, but that noise had sounded natural, animal. This cough was human—weak and tiny and all alone—and she worried that it would locate her, give her position away entirely. She swallowed hard, biting back the burn of mucus in her lungs.

With the moon, she could see the woods more clearly. See for certain that everything was just as she'd suspected—empty, abandoned, dead leaves, dead trees. This was when the snow started. She felt it first on her scalp, put her fingers to her head and was surprised to feel wetness. Bringing her hands to her face, she could see the snow where it combined with the blood from the cuts on her hand, thinning it, spreading it. She looked up and the snow hit her face, wet, cold, clean.

She chose a tree at the edge of the small clearing, one from which she could still see the moon. She wrapped herself around the base of it, covering herself in leaves—her legs first, then her chest, then her face. Then finally burrowing her arms under, all of her hidden by the leaves, all but a tiny opening for her eyes to watch the moon, to watch and wait for the moon to disappear and for the sun to re-announce itself and for everything to go back to normal.

ONE OF TWO THINGS might have happened at this point. Either she waited as long as she could before getting scared and returning to the car. Or, she stayed where she was, letting the snow pile steadily on top of her. She would have fallen asleep not knowing that her legs and arms had already lost feeling. As the nerves shut down, there would have been a sensation of burning, of fire in her fingers and toes, the end of awareness.

Her heartbeat slowed. The leaves froze to her body. The snow piled steadily. She concentrated on the near-imperceptible pressure of leaves on top of her. It felt like comfort. It didn't feel like giving up. By morning she would have been dead. They wouldn't have found her even if they'd known to look for her there.

A late-winter thaw would have done nothing but loosen her body from the tree base, send it slowly down the hill into the river close by. She hadn't seen it because of the ice and leaves. She hadn't known how close she'd come to the riverbank. Maybe if she'd found the water, she could have followed it back to civilization. Maybe. But she hadn't.

Her body wouldn't have floated. She'd have been hooked by branches, pulled under by the flotsam. Just another piece of jetsam that, when it did finally wash to shore, washed up only as a femur, a patella, a sliver of mandible maybe. "A dog bone," someone might have guessed before throwing it back into the river. "How sad," they would have said aloud, imagining the dog on the ice, imagining it going down, the struggle, the fear. "How very, very sad." Not once would they have thought of Nora Lindell, the missing girl from three towns over, two full counties away.

AND THEN THERE'S THE chance that she thought of all this. That, lying there, she thought of all the grisly things that we would one day think. She thought, death by ice, or brutalization by this young man in this strange car with the possibility of escape or even return? Damaged goods, she thought, damaged but alive.

Perhaps she found her way back to the car more easily than she'd expected. Uphill, breathing heavily. Perhaps very little time had passed. She was sweating. She wanted to take off her sweater, but she knew better, knew that it was merely a trick being played by her body.

She heard the car before she saw it. And before

that, she smelled it. Smelled the gasoline, thick and strange in the cold snowy air. She was surprised to feel relief. Surprised to feel less scared now that she was back in his company.

He would have laughed when he saw her. He would have reached across the seat, just as he'd done earlier in the day outside the Greyhound station. "Figures," he would have said, pushing the door open, making room for her on the passenger side.

And Nora, somehow different already, somehow resigned, would have scooted in next to him and asked for a cigarette.

OR MAYBE SHE DIDN'T get out of the Catalina at all because he never took her to the woods. And he never took her to the woods because he'd never had anything but good intentions. Maybe when she got into his car that day at the bus station, he asked her immediately where she wanted to go, and maybe just as quickly she told him the airport. Just like that. They were both confused by the suddenness of it all, confused but also pleased. Maybe he laughed at her and maybe she laughed with him, so that he was charmed by her brazenness. And just like that he decided to do it. He decided to drive this complete stranger to the airport just because he could. Perhaps he was returning a favor once done for him.

At most she thanked him. Not effusively, but quickly, curtly.

"Where will you go?" he might have asked.

"Argentina," she might have said. "Russia, India. Who knows?"

He nodded.

"Unless you have suggestions?" she said, her question perhaps a way to postpone getting out of the car; to postpone the reality of being on her own for the first time.

"I've always liked Arizona," he said.

"The Grand Canyon," she said. "Of course."

"It's just a thought," he said. He shrugged and looked at his hands where they rested on the steering wheel. An airplane passed overhead, the sound of its engine large and deep.

Nora nodded. She put her hand on his shoulder. It was the first and only time she touched him. "Thank you," she said.

"Don't mention it," he said and laughed—the whole thing impossible, unlikely.

When she was out of the car, standing on the curb, leaning down into the passenger window of the Catalina, the skirt of her uniform flying up in the

November air, she said, "Will you get in trouble for this?"

He shook his head, laughed again. "I don't even exist," he said. "How can something that doesn't exist get in trouble? It's been the story of my life. One day here. One day there."

She laughed too, not actually understanding. He rolled up the window and she stood up straight; she stomped her feet and shoved her hands into her armpits for warmth. The Catalina pulled away. She didn't go inside till it was completely out of sight.

IT WAS AFTER MIDNIGHT and Halloween was technically over, but some flight attendants were still wearing costumes. Nothing fancy, nothing that conflicted with their regulation uniforms, but a few women were wearing half-masks. It was a chance to see what Martha Washington and Marie Antoinette would have looked like as stewardesses.

"You're a schoolgirl," said the stewardess dressed as Marie Antoinette. Nora looked down at her uniform, worrying possibly that she'd been caught so soon. "I tried to come up with a way to be a schoolgirl, but it's hard with this suit," the stewardess said. "So I settled on Marie Antoinette." The woman pointed to the mask as if Nora might have missed it. Nora nodded. The stewardess didn't leave. Perhaps she sensed something strange, after all.

"I thought you might have been Josephine," said Nora.

"Who?"

"She probably had Napoleon's baby. She hated him, but she was beautiful." Nora looked down at her plaid skirt. "Anyway, I borrowed my little sister's uniform. It's a hand-me-down. I used to wear it when I was in school, if you can believe that."

WE DON'T KNOW IF Nora Lindell even went to the airport or if she ever got on a plane. But the local newspaper really did run a piece shortly after Halloween in which Tracy Hinckley, twenty-three, single stewardess and mother of one, was quoted as having talked to a girl in a uniform who fit Nora's description.

"She was pretty," said Ms. Hinckley. "She looked my age. I thought she was my age. The way she talked." When asked about the uniform and why it wasn't a red flag, Ms. Hinckley said, "It was Halloween. There were lots of costumes. I was in costume myself, actually." There was a photo of Ms. Hinckley in her stewardess suit holding up a mask for the cameraman. "Josephine," she was quoted as saying. "Napoleon's lover. She was very beautiful."

.   .   .

TECHNICALLY, IT WAS JACK Boyd and not Trey Stephens who was the last to find out Nora was missing, because Jack Boyd was on his way back from visiting his biological father in Texas when the rest of us got word. Jack claimed to have seen Nora at the airport in Houston on the morning after Halloween. He had the unbelievable audacity to insist he had talked to her between terminals.

"I was visiting my dad," he told her.

"I'm visiting my grandmother," was her alleged reply.

"You're wearing your uniform?" he said.

"It's my costume," she said.

He nodded. "My dad's getting remarried," he said. "Just found out today."

Jack Boyd's flight was leaving soon and though they didn't talk long, it was long enough for Nora to reveal that she had a grandmother in Phoenix. She was only connecting in Houston.

While it was true that Mr. Boyd was getting remarried—for the fourth though not final time—Jack's airport run-in with Nora sat uneasily with the rest of us. Our own allegations had never been so specific, so daring as to include actual conversation. We especially didn't like that the article featuring the decidedly not-beautiful Tracy Hinckley came out *after* Jack Boyd had told us his story.

When we thought no one was listening, we asked our mothers about the Lindells, whether or not there was family out West. "Maybe in Arizona?" we asked. But they scoffed at us, shooed us away into other rooms, anywhere but the kitchen where we were only in their way. Our curiosity, they said, bordered on obsession.

NINE YEARS LATER, DANNY Hatchet had the bright idea to ask Sissy about the rest of her family—a grandmother, perhaps.

"No family anywhere but me and my dad," she said. It was January. There was snow. It was a chance run-in on the sidewalk a few blocks from the three-story Tudor—Sissy was in town only for the holidays. She was in her early twenties; Danny had just turned twenty-five.

Maybe he was high or maybe he just couldn't help himself. He said, "So what was it like? All those years?"

"What was it like?"

"Yeah," he said. He shoved his foot into the snow at his feet. He looked down. He felt foolish. He hadn't had a steady job in months. We knew this because our mothers told us, because Mr. Hatchet had told them.

"I'm still trying to figure that out," Sissy said. "Do you know what I mean?"

According to Danny, they went for drinks. He ordered bourbon, but she insisted on tequila. "Tequila or I'm leaving. That means you too."

They drank for hours. It's possible they played a few games of pool. She would have been handy with a cue. All the girls in our neighborhood had been. Too many basements, too many pool tables not to be good. Sarah Jeffreys had been one of the best—Sarah, whose rape he probably still felt responsible for, though it hadn't been Danny who raped her. He and Sarah had gone out a few times. They'd done a few things. He liked her and, for all we knew, she liked him. But when he found out about the rape, he changed. He felt responsible for the things men were capable of. We tried to understand, but at most we simply felt bad for both of them.

At some point, Danny had the wherewithal to ask Sissy about Phoenix. The city came back to him, making a path through the haze of cigarette smoke and the rush of alcohol. "Did you ever consider looking in Arizona?"

Sissy laughed. She was still sexy as a high schooler, but she'd turned unfriendly, brittle. "You're serious? You're seriously asking me this question right now?"

"Don't you have a grandmother out there or something?"

"My god," she said. There was spit in her laugh.

"You all thought of everything, didn't you?" She finished a final drop of tequila and wiped her mouth. Her hair was more orange than he remembered. "No," she said. "No grandmother in Phoenix. Like I said, no family anywhere."

They had sex in the back of Danny Hatchet's Nissan. It had belonged to his dad. It smelled like an ashtray. There was a banana peel on the back floorboard. There were lottery tickets and glass coffee mugs with dried-out grinds at the bottom. There was a spoon with something like Coffee-mate congealed at its tip. Sissy didn't question this. She didn't question any of it. She simply crawled in after him and lifted up her skirt.

When it was done, Danny dropped her off at her car, a large luxury SUV, parked at the rear entrance to the mall. There were two car seats in the back. Danny didn't ask about that.

When Sissy was safely outside the Nissan, she ducked her head down and looked at Danny. She was putting on a pair of white leather gloves. "Tell your friends," she said before she closed the door. "Tell them all. They'll want to know."

We didn't see Sissy again until Mr. Lindell's funeral and then not again until Minka Dinnerman's funeral, which would prove to be the last time any of us but Danny would ever see her, but that was years—almost a decade—in the future.

Shortly after Danny's alleged run-in with Sissy, a

for-sale sign went up on the lawn of the three-story Tudor. A moving van came. Danny called first; he was always calling these days. He needed money still, though he never exactly asked and we never exactly offered. "Stop by sometime soon," we said. "Well, no, not right now," we were forced to add. "The kids are home and the baby's a mess. The holidays and all. Yes, yes. Soon. Can't wait." To keep us on the phone, he told us about Sissy. "In the parking lot?" we said. "In the backseat of your dad's Nissan?" We closed our eyes. We pictured the exact parking spot where her SUV must have waited. We didn't believe him, and yet.

Our mothers called next. Mr. Lindell was finally leaving, they said. He was off to live with his daughter somewhere out West.

"Out West?" we asked. "Are you sure?"

"Out West," they said. "And why not? Some place with altitude where his knees won't hurt. You might think about something like that for us, you know."

"We know, we know," we said, our first and second daughters and sons crying in the background. "By the way," we said, trying to sound unconcerned, uninterested, "do you know anything about a baby, maybe two? Did Sissy get married? Are there twins?"

"Oh, enough," they said, upset that we hadn't offered them Denver, Lake Tahoe, or at the very least Truckee. "Hush up about the Lindells already."

It was Sissy, fourteen, who—exactly one year after her sister disappeared—led Kevin Thorpe, eighteen, into the mudroom. She took him by the hand at Sarah Jeffreys' Halloween party and led him to the mudroom off the rear garage. It was her idea and it was that simple. Kevin didn't force her to go in there, regardless of what anyone else might say.

Girls who saw them go off together said she was too easy. They said having a sister go missing turned Sissy into a tramp. "It's not her fault," they said. "But still." We might have pointed out to the girls that they—and not Sissy—were the ones dressed as skimpy bunny rabbits, as trashy vampires who'd just gotten out of bed, as season-impaired police officers. We might have, but we didn't. We knew they were hoping for our attention, but we had a hard time getting over how ridiculous they looked shivering in the winter chill, their determination to look sexy preventing them from dressing for the weather.

Of course, we knew Sissy wasn't a tramp because we knew Kevin Thorpe would be the first to be alone with her. We'd been keeping track. We had, in fact, been watching her since the day her sister disappeared. Probably we were filled with the desire to shake Kevin Thorpe's hand and then punch him in the face. Trey Stephens had gotten Nora, and now Kevin Thorpe was getting her little sister. It wasn't fair, and we said so under our breath.

"So it goes," said Chuck Goodhue, who then ran off to tell Paul Epstein because he knew it would break Paul Epstein's heart.

SISSY LIKED THE KISSING, at least according to Minka Dinnerman, who'd been her best friend since lower school. She'd told Minka it was wet and soft and alien. She said it took her out of herself and brought her back into herself all at once. According to Minka, there'd been a lot of talking, as well as kissing, which Minka thought was weird and she'd said so to Sissy. Their nine-year friendship didn't last the month of November.

"I just want to kiss you," Sissy had said in the mud-room, giggling at her own shamelessness.

"I just want to touch you," Kevin Thorpe had said, and maybe she'd felt sexy when he said it. Maybe she'd thought he was being flirtatious.

They kissed more. He backed up, pulling her with him, over to an old sofa. He sat down. She stayed standing. He put his hands on the waistline of her jeans. She put her hands on top of his, pulled them away.

"Sit down with me," he said.

She sat down, tucked her legs beneath her the way Nora used to sit when boys were around. This way Sissy was a little higher than Kevin, and probably she felt slightly more in control despite the age difference, despite the fact that he was a year older than Nora even, or older than Nora would have been.

He pulled her face towards his and she liked it. She liked being moved around.

"I like the way you manhandle me," she said. The line was from a movie maybe, she couldn't remember. She felt impossibly sexy.

"I like the way you won't shut up," he said.

She giggled. This went on for some time. The kissing, the back and forth. Both of them sitting, never lying down, but constantly repositioning.

After awhile he went for her pants again, and again she moved his hands away.

"You're good at that," he said.

"Thank you," she said. It felt like play. It felt like what it was supposed to feel like. But then he put his hands on her pants again, and this time she felt her face get hot.

"We can't have sex," she said.

He laughed at her. "I wasn't going to have sex with you," he said.

She felt her face get hotter. She felt young suddenly. She said, "Oh," and moved back away from him a little.

"You're embarrassed," he said.

"I'm embarrassed," she said.

"You're also cute," he said. He put his hands on either side of her face. She felt small in those hands and she liked it. He smiled at her. She liked that too.

"Kiss me again," she said.

He did, but he moved his hands from her face and she heard the sound of a belt buckle, not her own. She didn't look down; she just kept kissing him, her face getting hotter, the heat spreading to her chest.

She felt his hands on top of hers. She squeezed them. He squeezed hers back. He pulled them towards him, towards his pants, and what she felt was soft and not soft at the same time. This detail Minka was sure of, because she'd thought the same thing a month earlier when she and Marty Metcalfe spent seven minutes in a closet together. And, like Minka, Sissy claimed to know what she was feeling; she'd heard Nora talking with her friends before. She knew what was happening, and yet she'd said she felt something like homesickness in the bottom of her stomach.

He kept his hands on top of hers, moving them as he wanted them to be moved. The whole time he kissed her, and this is what she tried to concentrate on. Whenever he took his hands away, she stopped, and he had to put his hands back in order to get hers to move again. It wasn't complicated, but it also wasn't easy.

After awhile, he said, "You can put your mouth on it." He said this while he was kissing her, and she couldn't understand him, and she said so.

"What?" she said, his mouth on top of hers. "What did you say?"

He pulled back a little, said, "You can put your mouth on it if you want to."

This is when she stood up. She was shaking her head. She couldn't speak.

"Wait, Sissy," he said. "Just wait." His hand was on her waistline again, pulling at the button and zipper, pulling the fabric down.

"Just let me see it," he said. "Just let me see it."

She looked away and he pulled the fabric down hard, just enough so that her pubic hair was exposed.

He made sounds. She closed her eyes. One hand held down her pants, the other hand was around himself, working.

"Look at it," he said.

She looked at his face instead, but she was crying a little, hoping it would be over, wanting him to have whatever he needed to finish. His eyes were closed.

"Look at it," he said again. She did, even though he wouldn't have known. She looked and she felt dizzy, felt like she was being held up only by the hand holding down her pants.

"Sissy, Sissy, Sissy," he leaned back his head, eyes still closed. "Sissy, Sissy, Sissy. Sit on it," he said. "Just sit on it."

She turned away and saw, standing not four feet away, Mrs. Jeffreys in the doorway of the mudroom. Neither the girl nor the woman spoke. Mrs. Jeffreys was crying, a detail only Sissy knew, one she would refuse to reveal for years—even to Minka—out of respect for Mrs. Jeffreys or out of shame for what she'd done or maybe simply because admitting Mrs. Jeffreys' tears would require admitting her own. Whatever the reason, the sight of Mrs. Jeffreys and her wet, crumpled face was enough to stop Sissy from crying.

Another detail Sissy kept to herself for years was the fact that she'd seen her sister late on the night she disappeared, much later than anyone else. She'd knocked on her bedroom door and when Nora didn't answer, Sissy let herself in. She was surprised, but only partly, to see her older sister under the bed, under the mattresses actually; Nora had taken out the slats that kept them elevated and now she was beneath them— the weight of the box spring and mattress fully on top of her. Her head was turned towards the door. Her eyes were open.

"What are you doing?"

"Killing myself," Nora said.

"Should I tell Dad?"

"No."

"Can I borrow your fangs?"

"Top drawer to the right," Nora said.

Sissy found the fangs, stood in front of her sister's vanity, and put them on.

"Can you breathe?"

"More than I want," said Nora.

"Do you want me to sit on you?"

"Maybe next time."

"Lights on or off?"

"Off."

It would be wrong to say that Sissy didn't think about this often. But it would also be wrong to say that she assigned it any significance other than that it was the last time she saw her sister and that it was a cruelly meaningless last memory.

SISSY LOOKED AT KEVIN. He hadn't heard the door open, didn't know they weren't alone. He was still saying Sissy's name, still enticing her to sit on it. Very gently, she undid Kevin's grasp on the waistline of her pants. She rested his hand on his knee, which is when he opened his eyes. At first all he saw was Sissy, at least that's what he would say later, glorifying the moment. "She looked like a fucking goddess on fire," he said. "All that red hair. Shit." But then he saw Mrs. Jeffreys, and Mrs. Jeffreys, seeing that he was finished, felt at liberty to speak.

"Zip your fly," she said. "Kevin Thorpe, zip your fly." Mrs. Jeffreys was still crying, but she stood up straight, refusing to leave them alone. She held out her hand. "Sissy," she said. And Sissy, everyone's favorite little sister, went to her. She put her hand in Mrs. Jeffreys' and together they left the mudroom, left the party, and walked to the foot of the cul-de-sac to the three-story Tudor where Mr. Lindell lay on a couch, not knowing that his fourteen-year-old daughter was only a few blocks away, under the escort of Mrs. Jeffreys.

In ten different ways, on that interminable three-block walk, Mrs. Jeffreys promised Sissy that she had no choice but to rat her out to her father. The entire walk, in fact, she said that she owed it to Mr.

Lindell to tell him what Sissy had done. That even if she wanted to keep it a secret, she couldn't. It was her responsibility as a parent, as a mother. Sissy said nothing, but clutched at Mrs. Jeffreys' hand and listened as she talked.

"What I wish is that nothing had happened. What I wish is that there was nothing to tell. The position you put me in. Can you imagine? Oh, Sissy."

At the front door of the Tudor, Mrs. Jeffreys stopped talking. She turned Sissy towards her, looked her up and down, and said, "Who are you supposed to be, anyway? What's your costume?"

Sissy looked down as if trying to figure out the answer. She looked at her hands, then at the sleeves of her shirt. She remembered finding the flannel western in the bottom drawer of Nora's bureau. She remembered spending the entire afternoon just trying to find a few pieces of clothes in her sister's drawers that would fit her. She remembered holding up Nora's earrings one at a time, before deciding on a pair to wear to the party.

"I'm Nora," Sissy said finally and held up her arms, as if motioning to her entire body. "See?"

Mrs. Jeffreys shook her head, tried to hold back tears. "You poor thing," she said, then rang the doorbell. "You poor, poor thing."

Of course, when Mr. Lindell answered the door,

exactly what Sissy had thought would happen, happened. She was handed over. Mr. Lindell didn't ask. Mrs. Jeffreys didn't offer. The latter returned to the party, where she officiated that much more closely, and the next day Mr. Jeffreys installed a lock on the outside of the mudroom, as if taking away the place would also take away the instinct.

Sissy went upstairs to her sister's bedroom, closed the door, climbed under the bed, and lowered the mattresses on top of her. Mr. Lindell went back to the couch. They kept the lights off and, like this, they passed the anniversary of Nora's disappearance.

Sarah Jeffreys was twelve years old when she got into the backseat of Franco Bowles' Dodge. They were neighbors. They'd grown up together—if you can say that a twelve-year-old and a nineteen-year-old can grow up together. But they'd lived on the same block, gone to the same pool parties—those ageless affairs where mothers and fathers and high schoolers tolerated the company of middle schoolers, even lower schoolers, because they were related, because it passed the hour, the day, the summer. Time needed to be passed, days needed to go by. Pools needed to be swum, skin tanned, bellies fed. One pool party ended and the next was planned. It was that simple, that easy, that fun. And by the end of the summer, the fun was so monotonous that we were thankful for it to be over, for school to have begun again.

In this way, then, you can say that Franco Bowles and Sarah Jeffreys grew up together. She was in the shallow end when he was in the deep end, but they were in the same water. She was closer to Tommy Bowles, of course, because of their age. But she knew that at night when the families were reunited— when brothers were returned to sisters, and children returned to parents—Tommy went with Franco and the two of them went with Mr. and Mrs. Bowles and the four of them crossed the street together to the gaudy two-story Colonial across the street with what some of our mothers referred to as an unnecessary and showy addition.

In all those summers, at all those pool parties, there'd been nothing special between Sarah and Franco, not that we'd seen. There'd been no inappropriate flirtation, no quick aside in the bushes, no rumors of the two of them accidentally overlapping in one of the changing rooms. Nothing. And when Franco left for college, it was no different for Sarah than when any other neighbor's older sibling left that year. She didn't pine his absence. She didn't even say goodbye.

That fall we entered seventh grade, and Sarah, like

almost every other seventh-grade girl, realized that we paid a little more attention if she rolled her skirt a time or two at the top. Just one or two more inches exposed at the knee and we were done for. And Sarah liked the attention. Every girl liked the attention—it's true—but Sarah was willing to talk to us, to flirt with us. She added an extra wiggle when she walked, an extra half skip to every step that allowed the skirt to rise just a centimeter more in the wind, and that centimeter made Sarah a sort of darling among us—Danny, Winston, Drew, Chuck, Stu Zblowski (who named every dog he was ever given after himself, which was either really strange or really awesome), even Trey Stephens admitted she was somehow sexier than the others.

The thing about Sarah was that she'd never even kissed a boy. At least not any boy that we knew about, and we would have known about it if it had been any of us. We were boys, after all, which means we were creeps—our mothers' word—which means we were indiscreet and couldn't help ourselves when it came time to trading what we'd done or not done or when and with whom and how.

Wasn't it Jack Boyd who put his fingers in our face after putting his hands down Lily Bunker's pants one night? And wasn't it Chuck Goodhue who liked the idea so much that he stopped washing his hands, insisting that the only way to measure the day when he went to bed at night was to hold his hands to his face and breathe the evidence of everything that had or hadn't happened? God, we were creeps! But children also, which is what makes it excusable—excusable but perhaps for this reason also frightening, disconcerting that there wasn't someone there saying no, stop, don't do that. At least don't do that *yet*. But there wasn't. There was only each other, us; Chuck Goodhue was Winston Rutherford's gauge, and Trey Stephens was Danny Hatchet's, and so on. Our only limitation was our imagination, and that school year—and every school year after—our imaginations seemed to grow, to outdo what we'd ever believed possible. We outran our wildest fantasies. That is, until Nora Lindell went missing, and the only fantasy we could ever conjure suddenly involved her or some aspect of her, like her little sister.

IF WE LOST SARAH Jeffreys after high school—lost her in a more euphemistic way than we lost Nora Lindell—then seventh grade was the year we found her. It was the year before the rape, when she was always around, at every basement party, at every truth-or-dare. Always the instigator, never the disciple. It was the year she got not just good with a pool cue, but really good. She was a guy's girl, which is maybe why the other girls didn't relate to her. We liked her too much; they couldn't be her friend, they could only be jealous.

She was ahead of us all in some ways. What's clear now is that she knew what it would take years for the rest of us to learn—that none of it mattered, that all of the ins and outs and chagrins of childhood were meaningless. What mattered was what was ahead, so fuck it. Do it, say it, be it. She was a go-getter and that scared the hell out of us, but it also intrigued us, as did the fact that the other girls steered clear of her. And so of course she became the girl we championed. How could she not?

The summer after seventh grade was the summer Sarah discovered cutoffs. Chuck Goodhue used to clutch his heart when she walked by and say, "I'm a goner, boys. Those legs are going to do me in." Chuck was the son of a merciless flirt, the kind of dad who might pull you aside and say, "If you love her, let her kill you, kid. My god, look at the melons on that one." Merciless and completely inappropriate. Chuck, of course, was Mr. Goodhue's best mimic.

It's funny now to think back on the image of that underweight and acne-covered boy, grabbing at his chest like an old man. But at the time, his pantomime made sense to us. We felt it just the same in our own chests, maybe even stronger. That feeling was life or death, all or nothing, and truly, truly we believed our summer depended on the frequency and length of Sarah Jeffreys' cutoffs.

Even now it's unclear exactly how or why the events in the backseat of Franco Bowles' Dodge occurred. Because charges were never pressed, because nothing was ever confirmed, because our gossip was always shushed by whichever mother was closest, we were never able to put it all together. We could never confirm or deny the theory that Franco was an incurable pervert any more than we could confirm or deny the chance that the entire incident was an accident, a misunderstanding, a misstep that might have been avoided.

All we knew—all we know—is that Sarah wasn't the same after getting into the Dodge. Sarah wasn't the same, Franco left town, and Mr. and Mrs. Bowles didn't attend a single pool party the summer before our eighth-grade year. Tommy was allowed to attend, perhaps even forced by his parents. Probably they knew that his presence would keep us from ever being able to sort out what really happened. That was the summer Tommy's face got so sunburned it boiled, and ever after he blushed at even the slightest mention of flirtation or girls or sex, as if his skin never fully healed from that one summer's burn. Punishment, somehow, for his brother's trespass.

When school started the next fall, we noticed the

other girls were nicer to Sarah. She made friends with the cheerleading squad and eventually joined. Senior year she was captain. Her mother made sure the best parties happened at Sarah's house. And after Nora Lindell disappeared, there were times when we actually forgot that Sarah had been compromised. Almost every single one of us dated her at some point. The one thing we refused to say was whether we'd all also had sex with her, though by the time we graduated, it's probable that at least a half dozen of us had.

Danny Hatchet was the one who took the little time he actually got to spend with her the most seriously. He was the first to go on a real date with Sarah, and was somehow unaware of the rape. Blame the fog of medication his doctors kept him on. Who knows? But somehow Danny alone made it through eighth grade without knowing what everyone else seemed to know.

It was ninth grade, the year Mrs. Hatchet would eventually kill herself, when, out of nowhere, Danny approached Sarah at lunch one day and asked her on a date. Just like that. He put his pill bottles back in his lunch bag, took a final swig of chocolate milk, and walked over to Sarah's table without saying a word to any of us about what he was doing. We were torn between thinking Danny was a retard and a god.

Lily Bunker was there when it happened—was,

in fact, sitting right next to Sarah—and she'd tried to answer for her. She'd said, "I don't think so, Danny," not in a mean way, more in a sympathetic way, like she was looking out for someone who happened to lack common sense. And being girls, a few of them at the table giggled and, okay, maybe from where we were sitting, a few of us giggled too out of sheer nervousness. But Danny, somehow the least embarrassed of all of us, said, "Okay," and turned to walk back towards us. Again, retard or god? We couldn't tell, but we were, at that moment, in awe.

It sounded like a mouse squeaking when Sarah finally spoke. Danny had already turned away from her and so was forced to walk back to the table of girls, none of them giggling now, and say, "What?" And Sarah, just like that, said, "Yeah, okay. Sounds good."

We watched the girls and the girls watched us. It was the beginning of something, an opening in the doorway. We eyed them in wonder and they eyed us in disbelief. This date between Sarah and Danny felt like a secret between the ninth-grade girls and the ninth-grade boys. Suddenly, we were complicit. Suddenly, we had something to talk to them about. It was the true beginning of adolescence, the change we'd been waiting for, and it was all because Danny Hatchet, our weirdo friend in the sweatshirt, had decided to ask the only girl that we knew for a fact had been hurt already on a date.

IT'S LIKELY MRS. HATCHET put him up to it. It's likely Mrs. Hatchet recognized Sarah's internal scars and was trying to preempt the girl from turning out the same way—sensitive, frazzled, unhinged. Which is not to say that Mrs. Hatchet was taken advantage of in her youth or even messed with, which is also not to say that she wasn't. We don't know. What we know is she was a skittish woman who, just before Thanksgiving our ninth-grade year, locked herself in the garage and started her car. How could she not have seen a kinship—from however far away—in Sarah Jeffreys?

Danny Hatchet didn't find out about the rape until after they'd crawled under the pool table in his basement, until after he'd forced his hand down her pants. He found out not because Sarah objected to his hand, but because when he told us about it, Chuck Goodhue called him a fucking idiot and then repeated the story of Franco Bowles and the backseat of his Dodge.

What we remember about that day is the way Danny kind of closed his eyes while Chuck was talking, the way his face eventually fell forward and into his hands. When he finally looked up all he said was, "I should go home. Sorry." And for the rest of high school Danny did act sorry, like it was his job to apologize for not only Franco, but for all of us, for men in general.

We didn't try to comfort him when he went home that day. We didn't try to tell him that everything would be okay, because we didn't think it would be. What's funny is that he actually went on a few more dates with Sarah. For a couple weeks it looked like maybe they were right for each other–as right as two ninth-graders can be. But then Danny's mom died and his dad started drinking again and, just like that, he stopped calling Sarah. Probably he thought he was being nice. Probably he thought she didn't want anything to do with a kid whose mom was so crazy she had to kill herself, whose dad was such a fuckup he had to drink himself to sleep every night.

CHUCK GOODHUE DATED HER next, and Marty Metcalfe after that. It's sad, because we all genuinely liked her; we all remembered that one glorious school year when Sarah was nothing but confidence and moxie. But what's really sad is that Danny Hatchet was probably the only one who really cared for her, was the only one of us who genuinely seemed to understand her, which is funny–right?–because what could a ninth-grader really have understood about another ninth-grader? And there's a good chance he was the only one of us that she ever really cared for.

But life got in the way, and ultimately Danny couldn't cope with what another boy had done, and after graduation, Sarah disappeared. We think she went to college, though somehow not one of us—not even Danny—ever seemed to ask which one. Her mother and father left town, moved someplace coastal. Our mothers mentioned a house that one of them had inherited. And that was the end of Sarah. We'd been too busy with Nora Lindell to understand that they were just biding their time until high school was over—feigning normalcy as best they could, as if leaving before graduation would have undermined any chance Sarah still had for complete recovery—and they could leave the mid-Atlantic behind, leave all of us behind. And from time to time we now remember—alone in our bathrooms, shaving before going in to work—that while that memory comes and goes for the rest of us, the backseat of Franco Bowles' Dodge is something that Sarah will never forget.

A fter school, walking home, we would make snack stops at the various houses of our friends. Mrs. Epstein's for Rice Krispie treats, Mrs. Price's for bananas and peanut butter, Mrs. Rutherford's for cake batter, Mrs. Hatchet's—before she died—for fruit roll-ups or Coca-Cola gummy bottles (nothing was ever from-scratch in that house, everything store-bought, pre-made). Mrs. Dinnerman's house wasn't really good for snacks—at most there was a bowl of fruit on the kitchen table—but we went there anyway just to see her.

Minka Dinnerman's mother had been imported from the old world sometime in the seventies. Supposedly, it was Mr. Dinnerman himself who brought her back from a business trip to Russia. This seems unlikely, since Minka's dad never showed much initiative at anything other than importing Mercedes, but that's how our mothers explained her arrival and that's where the story stands. A full-fledged Soviet, a cold warrior, Mrs. Dinnerman liked to scold us when we asked about St. Petersburg. "Leningrad," she would say. "My home is Leningrad."

We would mimic her and spit would fly from our mouths, the vitriol somehow inherent in the language. *Leningrad.* Impossible to say without a snicker sneaking through.

"I can tell of you about Leningrad, little boyz. I can tell of you many things that you should not know. Do you want to know of about dead babies? I can tell you of about dead babies in tiny glass bottles. Seven-headed babies." She frowned. "We are collectors. It is true. We are a country of collectors. Do not talk to me about Peter."

We steered the conversation away from Russia, towards snacks and the fruit bowl in the center of her kitchen table. We liked that she liked the fruit of our country, that she was, in fact, fascinated by its endless variety. We often had the impression that she'd never actually eaten any of it, but that she continued to buy it for its color, for its shape, for its size and smell and sponginess. "This color of green, boyz," she might say, running her finger down the edge of an apple or a watermelon. "This color ought to be ashamed of about itself. So slootry"—a combination, we assumed, of sultry and slutty—"so tempting. A prostitute of color." When we blushed, crisp, tingly bubbles of laughter came from her mouth and nose that seemed to confirm her own deliberate role as temptress.

If any of us had ventured to touch the day's chosen fruit, she would have slapped the audacious hand. The fruit was a display, not an offering. In the two decades she'd been in our country, she hadn't learned what snacks were, hadn't cared to learn. Doubtless this troubled Minka, kept her skinny and sickly and pale, but we loved Mrs. Dinnerman for it, for how decidedly *not* our mothers she was.

THE HOUSE—TWO-STORIED, GREEK REVIVAL, pink—smelled of mothballs and dill and eggs. The eggs alone should have kept us away, and the dill a nightcap to the boiled, fried, stewed sulfur of the eggs. But we didn't stay away.

She wasn't Jewish, which might have been a problem for Mr. Dinnerman's own mother had the Russian import not been so unapologetically attractive. "You will give me beautiful grandchildren," is what Mr. Dinnerman's mother said, and it was the closest either of them came to getting her blessing.

But Minka–Minka was decidedly not beautiful. It's not that she was unattractive; she just wasn't her mother. Mrs. Dinnerman was what you might call statuesque. She was six-one, velvet-skinned, honey-eyed, and blond. There is always a mother like this–a mother who eclipses not only all the other mothers, but the daughters as well. And the daughter who was hurt worst by this mother was, of course, Minka.

Maybe if Minka had been Mrs. Jeffreys' daughter or Mrs. Epstein's, we might have thought she was something special–a cute girl, perhaps, a sweet little piece of something. As it was, we could only see her as not–Mrs. Dinnerman. Minka was plain, round-faced, pale, inexplicably short, and undeniably Jewish. To her credit, she was athletic, which behooved our school but not our hearts. Her mother, on the other hand, was a klutz, a kind of off-kilter gazelle, and this only made us love her more.

DREW PRICE WAS THE only one with fast enough hands to ever dare reach across to the fruit bowl and rip grapes from the vine to throw them one by one–when Mrs. Dinnerman wasn't looking–into various corners of the kitchen. Sometimes she wouldn't notice them, but when she did, she would bend over and we would sigh with gratitude for that lovely Russian ass–round and high and firm. Again, thankfully, deliciously, nothing like our own mothers. And nothing, for that matter, like our female counterparts.

To be fair, we went to the Dinnermans' not just for the view, but also for the stories. Of all the mothers, Mrs. Dinnerman was the least tight-mouthed, the most unrestrained. She would talk about anyone, everyone. There were no boundaries. It was as if she didn't register that we were there, as if we'd caught her in the middle of a monologue that had started before we arrived and would continue once we'd left. Either that, or she didn't care that we were children. There was no distinction between us and our mothers or our fathers. There was only the fact that we weren't Russian, weren't her own, and because of that we didn't matter. Loyalty didn't exist for her in our language. Everything was public domain. Whatever the reason, we didn't care. We liked going and listening—to her stories, to her gossip, to her strange and terrifying way of speaking.

AT THE TIME IT never made sense to us—Trey Stephens' insistence that he didn't find Mrs. Dinnerman sexy—but looking back on it, we begin to understand. Women—adult women—would never hold him captive in the same way a girl—teenaged, yes, but a girl all the same—could preoccupy his mind.

We thought he was being tough, coy, all those

nights we stayed up late in his basement, sitting with our backs against the wall, our knees splayed in various directions, talking about Minka's mother.

"Nope, boys, she doesn't do it for me," he said.

"Bullshit," said Chuck Goodhue, his arms crossed over his chest, his hands sunk deep into his armpits. "Minka's mom does it for everyone." Funny that it would be Minka Dinnerman, not her mother, who would one day threaten the integrity of Chuck Goodhue's marriage.

"Seriously," said Stu Zblowski, whose parents had recently given him a yellow Lab that he'd naturally named Stu. "I'd consider naming my dog after her if she'd show me even one boob."

"Not for me," Trey said. "She's an oldie. That face. Makes me sick to think about looking at that face while I screw."

"Bullshit," again Chuck Goodhue.

Trey's final comeback: "Give me a girl in uniform any day."

Thirty years later those words, for those of us who remembered them, made us shiver.

AFTER NORA DISAPPEARED, MRS. Dinnerman's role in our lives changed slightly. We still visited her kitchen, still threw grapes onto her linoleum floors, still admired the perfect roundness of her foreign rear end. But we visited now to hear her version of Nora's fate. While the other mothers discouraged our fascination, Mrs. Dinnerman sought it out.

"I have a gossip, boyz." She waited for Minka to take her book bag upstairs; she never had gossips for Minka. "Do you want to hear my gossip?" Before we could answer: "Nora is not deed, boyz. The facts is no, Nora is not deed."

"Then where is she?" Paul Epstein often carried the conversation. Mrs. Dinnerman appealed to him, sure, but she didn't make him dizzy the way she made the rest of us. After all, he was already in love with Sissy by that time, already completely preoccupied with another female.

"Feh. And why would I know where she is? No, I do not know where she is, bet I know that when I go missing from my family house at sixteen, I do not go missing as deed. I go missing as alive and–" she pinched her lips together with her fingers, a gesture so sexy that its effect required most of us to cross our legs in a show of attempted decency "–as a wolunteer."

IT WAS DURING THESE afternoons with Mrs. Dinnerman–Minka and her friends, sometimes even Sissy, upstairs, safely out of earshot–that we learned about Mrs. Lindell, famously absent from our lives, famously absent and undeniably dead.

"She was *kraseevaya*, you know, beautiful."

Probably what we wanted to say was, "No, Mrs. Dinnerman, you're the beauty. We love you." But probably what we said was nothing. Probably we waited, sitting on her awful, tall stools, positioning and repositioning our feet, crossing and re-crossing our legs, for her to say something else.

"The mothers, *your* mothers, boyz, they were nice to her like they are nice to me." The sibilance in her speech was mesmerizing, snakelike and sharp. Russian, so very, very Russian. How strange and wonderful to be with a woman who understood her beauty and was not embarrassed by it. How very un-American. "Yes, I see you turning red, Chuck Gootyue. You know of what I am talking about." She wagged her finger in our directions. "They were nice to her only as of much as *patreeabny*, you know, as much as they must be."

Drew Price threw a grape on the floor. We listened to it bounce.

"When she is round," she made the shape of a baby in front of her, "they like her wery well because she no longer has her shape, you know. Because when she is not round," again the gesture in front of her own belly, "she has a wonderful shape."

She spotted the grape where it lay against the base of Danny Hatchet's stool. She picked it up, blew on it, and popped it in her mouth. Then she dusted off her hands and looked at us. "Bet den she die. Baby number two is too much baby for her. Out you go, boyz. Baby Minka and her papa must eat."

It's possible that, in Arizona, Nora Lindell's hair turned a burnt yellow. Her skin became a caramel color she'd never seen before. She aged quickly. She waited tables. She worked hard. She rented a trailer.

Nights, she sat in a folding chair set up on the dirt patch outside her home. She looked up at the sky and thought things like, "Tonight the sky is Arizona." Some nights, she might even have thought of us. She wondered which of us had graduated, which hadn't. She wondered who'd gotten into what schools. She thought about Trey Stephens, maybe, and whether he'd taken another girl to prom after all. Of course she thought of her father, her sister, but we didn't worry about that.

Most nights, she leaned back, closed her eyes, tried to imagine the things inside her. She could call them babies, because that's what they were. She could even call them daughters, because that's also what they were. Still, it seemed most right to leave them as heartbeats for now, nothing else struck true in Nora's brain. And, after all, heartbeats was how she saw them sitting there under that gaudy Arizona sky, her eyelids shut tight, her head turned upward, her eyes turned inward, southward, to look squarely at the things that were sharing that folding chair, sharing her body. What she saw was two heartbeats, red and bloody and tiny, tiny. Two little heartbeats perfectly and eerily syncopated. One heartbeat and then another.

What she saw clear as day were those two little heartbeat babies, and they each had exactly one arm and one hand, locked together at the fingers. Imagine something monstrous. Little red chimeras joined at the palm, floating there, not one thought in the world of anything other than themselves. Beastly organisms, selfish for existing in the first place. Sisters, she might have called them, and so defined them by each other and not by her. Because, more than anything, what Nora was sure of was that though they lived in her body, though she alone housed them while they grew, those babies didn't belong to her. They couldn't. She was still a child herself, after all. Still freckled and pig-tailed and awkward.

WE LIKED TO IMAGINE that she'd picked Arizona for the Grand Canyon and the warmth. Maybe she'd thought it was possible to live in it, in the canyon. But she never admitted that to anyone, not once she got there and saw how wrong her fantasy had been. The walls of Jack Boyd's bedroom were decorated with postcards of the Southwest. Postcards his father had sent while traveling with his fourth wife. We imagined Nora just beyond the postcards' borders. Always out of reach. These were the details of Arizona she now lived among. Open spaces; wood carvings and chalk draw-ings; gaping holes in the earth; grotesque protrusions upward out of the rock; and turquoise. Turquoise espe-cially. The turquoise was everywhere, and if anyone asked, she would have told them she'd gotten that right at least. The water was turquoise, the sky was turquoise, the jewelry was turquoise. And the people were so used to it they didn't even see it. The color was so common it was imperceptible. This was exactly what she wanted—to be in a place so unlike the one where she'd been born. Scorched earth, turquoise sky. Extremes.

She picked up waiting tables easily. She was good at it. The manager had said, "Have you waited tables before?" And Nora had shaken her head.

"Then why should I hire you?"

"I'm a blank slate," Nora said. "Teach me and I'll do exactly what you say."

"I like that," the woman had said. A woman just like you'd expect in a place like this. Tan, wrinkled, two parts chain smoker, one part beauty queen. She was soft somewhere deep down. She was a mother—of her own children, of course; but maybe also of Nora. Someone to guide her, show her how to live.

"You can start tomorrow," the woman had said.

"You should know I'm pregnant."

"Who isn't?"

BUT PROBABLY THERE WAS nothing friendly between the manager and Nora. Nothing unfriendly, either, but also nothing motherly as Nora might have hoped that first day. The cooks, though, would have been different. They would have taken to Nora immediately, and she almost immediately to them. At first they might have made her nervous, made her blush at the things they said and the way they said them. But soon the banter became something to go to work for, something to help pass the time.

They would have liked that she was pregnant, asking daily about the baby. When the bump grew, they might have asked to touch it. Of course she would let them.

"Babies," she had to remind them more than once. To the Mexican cook, she said *bambinos. Dos.*

"A baby having babies," he liked to say.

"Yes, yes," she said, already so much older and calmer than she should be. Already a woman, too much a woman. Seventeen, but also not seventeen. Our age, and yet a decade advanced.

SHE FELL FOR THE Mexican. The old man. She fell for the words he taught her, for the baby blanket he'd asked his sister to knit for him as a gift for Nora. She fell for his arthritis and his dark skin and the way he asked first about the babies and then about her. She fell, perhaps, too, for his food, for the cow tongue and the goat belly he brought her for lunch. But mostly, mostly she fell for the absence of sex.

He touched her cheek. She liked this. He held her hand. She liked this too. But even after she began spending nights with him, they did not have sex. Clothed in pajamas, they faced the window of his rancher and held each other. She in front, he in back. He held on to the babies and she held on to him.

A month before she gave birth, he asked her to marry him. For the first time, she was nervous.

"Why?" she said. "Why marry me?"

"For the girls," he said. "For all three of you. Let

me give you what I have." His sister had died. He'd been made head cook. His house was empty.

"What will change?" she said.

"Nothing will change. Crying babies, constant noises. We will not change." He overarticulated when he spoke. "I will give you your own bedroom." He looked down when he said this and blushed, because he did not like to talk about sex either and did not like the implication of her question.

She laughed then, laughed at him and with him. She put his hands on either side of her face and made his fingers pinch the skin. "Silly old man," she said. "Inheriting three silly young girls. I will marry you."

She left the restaurant and they moved her few belongings to the rancher. She insisted that the folding chair come with her, the one she'd first sat in under the Arizona sky.

"It is crap," he said, offended that she didn't think he could offer her better.

"My crap, though," she said.

"Americans and their crap," he said.

She set the folding chair up outside, in back by the swimming pool so that people driving by couldn't see it. She'd grown up with swimming pools, but she didn't tell him about that. She didn't want him to know he wasn't giving her something special. We'd all grown up with swimming pools. And we'd grown up with Nora Lindell. And sometimes, but only sometimes, she thought about this. When the babies kicked, especially, she thought about Trey Stephens and the way he ran his hands up and down her legs. Maybe she wished they were kicking him. She thought about Sissy only when the Mexican wasn't around. It was almost impossible to imagine her pale, fragile sister when there was someone so old and dark in the same room. It was almost impossible in fact to imagine another life, a different life, when he was there. And, after all, that's what she had married him for.

FOURTEEN YEARS AFTER NORA Lindell went missing, Jack Boyd claimed he saw her again, this time in the Phoenix airport. (This was five years after Sissy Lindell had confirmed to Danny Hatchet that there was definitely no family in Arizona; five years after she allegedly crawled into the backseat of his Nissan.) Jack said Nora looked older, just as he did. She had twins, he said, girls, maybe thirteen years old. This time he didn't talk to her.

He stopped at an airport pay phone, and the only person he could think to call was his mother.

"It's not her," Mrs. Boyd said.

"I'm watching her right now," he said. "It's Nora clear as day."

"That girl is dead," said Mrs. Boyd. "She died years ago and everyone knows it."

"There are three of them. One my age and two girls who look just like Sissy. Just like Nora and Sissy." He couldn't help laughing. "Goddamn twins."

Mrs. Boyd didn't believe it of course, but she couldn't help making the usual round of phone calls. Eighteen years of phone-tree etiquette had engrained it in her. She picked up the phone and started with the second mother on her list–Mrs. Hatchet, after all, was dead.

"Twins," she said to Mrs. Epstein. "Can you imagine?"

OUR MOTHERS TRIED, BUT we were the ones who really could imagine it. We were the ones who could picture those twins as if they were ours. We gave them the best of Nora. We gave them her hair–red, just as Jack Boyd had described. We gave them her poreless skin and her overabundance of freckles. We kept them slim, just as Nora and Sissy had been. Here and there, though, we added or subtracted a few inches. Paul Epstein kept them short, rounded their noses to look more like his mother's than like Nora's or Sissy's. Winston Rutherford would have given them well-defined chins. "The chin is a sign of character," he said to Maggie Frasier when he finally married her. He pointed to his own chin. "You can't fake that." He would have said this to Nora Lindell if she'd ever given him the chance. Drew Price, still not convinced Mr. Price wasn't his real father, no doubt had the twins closing in on six feet tall.

Jack Boyd didn't have the luxury of fantasy since, he insisted, he'd seen them for himself. But perhaps the real reason he couldn't imagine them as his own was because he could see too much of the man he suspected was the real father. Something he didn't admit for years, something he probably should have kept to himself, was that those two little red-haired girls had the undeniable and aggressive look of Trey Stephens. A savageness and confidence that, among us, only the public schooler had ever displayed. Those girls belonged to Trey, Jack Boyd finally confessed, some time after *Epstein v. Stephens* came to an end.

Jack was crying when he told us. We were drunk. Our wives were in the kitchen. Our daughters were huddled together in bedrooms on second and third stories. We were allowed, this once, to smoke our cigars inside in the basement. Jack put his hand on Paul Epstein's back. "Maybe if he'd known about his own girls, he wouldn't have touched yours," he said. We looked in other directions, trying hard to pretend we didn't know what he was talking about; trying hard to believe those twins weren't real, that Nora wasn't real anymore, that none of it was real—not even Paul's pain, and especially not the things that had happened to his daughter.

Nora Lindell was gone. And, with Trey Stephens in jail, he was gone, too, in a way. By this time, we'd already lost Minka Dinnerman and Mr. Lindell as well (a car crash and cancer, respectively). It seemed, some days, that life was nothing more than a tally of the people who'd left us behind.

Afternoons she spent in the pool with the girls. They were naturals in the water, just as she'd been. Just as Sissy had been. Evenings she spent in the kitchen, the windows open, the babies on a towel on the linoleum floor. She wore very little these days—a dress the weight of a slip, underwear, flip-flops. The breasts she'd grown while nursing had dried up, had shrunk smaller than the ones she'd arrived with in Arizona. She preferred it this way. It made her feel like the genderless thing that she'd wished all along she could be.

The babies were easy. They were good and simple. They preferred the Mexican to Nora, which Nora didn't mind because she, too, preferred the Mexican. Postpartum depression would have been too strong an expression, too dark, too complicated. There was no depression; there was simply a lack of connection, perhaps a lack of reality. In part, you could blame the fact that they were twins. They were so content with each other that it made sense for Nora to become more an overseer, a protector, than a mother. Most days, she was nothing more than a glorified babysitter or an affectionate but ultimately uninterested older sister.

The Mexican loved them all. It was from him that the girls would learn about love. Not that there wasn't a tenderness to Nora. There was. A great deal of tenderness, but it was the tenderness of a hospice nurse—of one committed to caring but too familiar with pain and parting to ever truly or fully invest.

LET'S SAY IT WAS a summer night. One that was uncharacteristically hot, even for Arizona. It was like this—it had to be like this—because heat alone—isolated, confined—can make a person crazy, can turn a good thing bad, if only for a moment. And don't forget that we like the Mexican. We like him because, like us, he loves Nora. He has cared for Nora and her two babies. So let's say it was hot. Let's say there was enough heat to excuse any sin, any crime, any transgression, just this once.

It was night. The babies were asleep. They'd been in their crib for several hours, fingers intermingled just as Nora had once imagined them when they were still womb-locked, body-bound. Perhaps they sucked on one another's thumbs that night, a habit they'd taken to only recently, one that turned Nora's stomach, though she couldn't explain why.

The house smelled like milk. It smelled like milk every night, the way that Chuck Goodhue's house smelled when his aunt and her new baby came to visit. Nora took refuge outdoors, poolside in her folding chair. She'd dived in just before midnight, the Mexican still not home, and she sat now with her legs stretched out before her, her wet hair hanging loose over the top of the chair, her underwear dripping wet, her tiny nipples hardened by the faintest breeze coming up through the mint garden.

She didn't hear the Mexican come in, but she saw the light from the kitchen hit the bank of the pool. At first nothing was different. Everything was the same. But when he opened the sliding glass door and waited in its frame, she understood.

"I am a man," he said.

"Yes," she said. "Of course."

He followed her to the bedroom. He was crying. She pulled down the sheet and got in bed, then she slipped off her underpants and turned away from him.

"Take off your clothes," she said.

"I am a monster," he said. Even drunk, he over-articulated.

"You are a man," she said.

It was fast, quiet.

Afterwards he turned away from her. It was Nora that held the Mexican that night. Their backs to the swimming pool, his back pressed into her chest, she held him, her hands locked tight against his stomach, just as he'd held her every night before the babies were born.

And Nora, possessing the bittersweet wisdom of

premature motherhood, already knew what we could only imagine, that the Mexican would be hurt more than she by these events, would be more humiliated, more embarrassed, more ashamed. Out of pride, disgrace, or some feeling too strong to bear in the company of others, the Mexican would want to leave her.

He was crying still. She squeezed a piece of his skin between her fingers.

"I am disgusting," he said.

She squeezed harder. "Don't go," she said. "Just please don't go away from us."

In the morning, he left her in bed alone and went to the babies. It was then—alone in bed, her body flat under a single white sheet—that she thought of Sissy, thought of Trey and her father and the three-story Tudor at the foot of the cul-de-sac. She didn't miss anything so mundane as her clothing or the television set and obviously not the swimming pool. What she missed presented itself in fragments, in images, incoherent and incomplete: Her mattress. The dark of her bedroom. Her sister's breath. The smell of her father's cologne in the morning. Things anyone would have missed: A bark from down the street. Leaves changing color. Leaves falling. Leaves existing at all. In particular she missed (or at least recalled with a slight gasp) the faint blue illumination from the fish tank in Trey Stephens' basement.

Danny Hatchet was a weird kid, always had been. He wore a sweatshirt all through summer, even on the hottest days. He kept it on at pool parties, like those fat kids who thought they were fooling everyone by keeping on their T-shirts at the ocean. But Danny wasn't fat, not even a little.

He was the kid always taking pills at lunch, the kid who pulled out brown medicine bottles and a small carton of chocolate milk from his lunch box instead of a sandwich and chips. He'd line up the bottles and open them one by one, and invariably we'd drop our heads into our hands and say, "Not this again. Gimme a fucking break. Enough with the pills already." But Danny took the pills daily, without ever taking any real notice of our remarks. First he'd drink the chocolate milk, then he'd pop in a pill, one at a time, over and over. He couldn't even get the order right—pill first, then the milk. That's the kind of kid he was. We asked him about that, about the order, and he said, like he was happy we had asked and even happier to be able to articulate a clear answer, "I don't like the taste of the pills. If I drink the milk first, then the pill never touches my tongue." He smiled when he said it, like he was proud to have completed a sentence. We shook our heads and waited for him to finish. We asked him about the chocolate milk, too, but he just grinned and took a sip. Every day with the chocolate milk. It was too much.

He picked his face during class, sometimes until it bled, and the teacher would excuse him even when he hadn't asked to be excused. He was always saying things like, "What'd I do? I don't get it." And, really, he didn't get it, you could just tell. There wasn't the willfulness in him to be a smartass. Teachers were always shaking their heads, saying things like, "Oh Danny. Enough already." Or, when he was apologizing for something he didn't understand, they might say, depending on their mood, something as snide as, "Yeah, you *are* sorry, Mr. Hatchet. You certainly are *sorry*." (Teachers were always calling us by our last names when they were mad or disappointed. Like it made it easier for them to tear us apart, break us down, if they pretended we were other adults.)

Our mothers were constantly making sure that Danny was included on weekends or summer vacations. "He doesn't have the same advantages that we have," they might say, trying to hide a slight gleam in their eyes. "He hasn't been as lucky." Words like *lucky* and *advantages* we knew, even at our young age, were upscale euphemisms for *not poor, not the son of a drunk* and, later, *not the son of a suicidal mother*.

Poor, by the way, is a relative term. The Hatchet house was as big as any of ours. They drove decent enough cars. (Remember the Nissan 300ZX his father brought home brand new during one of his many midlife crises? We were always groaning about who was going to have to sit in the trunk, but Danny—even though we usually made him take the shit seat—was always really excited when his dad was coming to get us, because he was coming in a sports car. But the sports car was a Nissan! They couldn't even get that right.)

At any rate, the point is, they went on vacations. They came to our clubs. What made them *poor* were the inconsistencies, the strange, inexplicable differences from how we lived, how we did things. The Hatchet house, for example, was not what our mothers would have called *well kept*. The paint was chipping; the bushes were overgrown; the lawn wasn't mown as often as it should have been. Mrs. Hatchet (who, at any given moment, seemed approximately five minutes away from crawling under a bed and crying her eyes out) installed lacey curtains when everyone else was putting in blinds. There were dust motes wherever there was sunshine strong enough to illuminate them. Their kitchen trash can never quite closed because the trash was always just a little too full. There were rooms with boxes that never got used (the rooms or the boxes). There were doors that we never saw opened—imagine that! The floors in the house were carpeted, and not just in the basement. Everything about Danny was slightly dirty, somewhat messy, and definitely a little bit smelly. He wore a patina of grime. A patina of gloom.

But in the end, Danny was Danny. He was weird, yeah, but he was one of us. And he must have known it. Because if there were longings in Danny to be at any school other than ours, we never saw it. Other than being a generally downtrodden-type kid, he never seemed especially to notice that he lived differently than we did. Like with his dad's Nissan. He genuinely believed that car was cool. And it never even occurred to him that we didn't feel the same way.

WHAT WE KNEW—WHAT NONE of us was supposed to know but what each of us knew because our mothers couldn't help themselves and so made us promise, one at a time, each believing she was the only mother spilling the beans and that it would never get around—was that Danny's grandmother footed the bill. She footed the bill for almost everything. She footed the bill for the Hatchets' house, their membership to the clubs, their annual Christmas trips up north, Mrs. Hatchet's prescriptions, Mr. Hatchet's spending sprees, and definitely Danny's education.

We had vague images of an old lady sitting by herself in a decaying mansion in New England, writing checks with Danny's name on them. As children, we were jealous of that old lady. We wanted her to be our grandmother. We wanted checks of our own. We wanted better vacations. The things we could have done with that money! What we believed was that Danny didn't know how to spend it, that Danny's family didn't know how to spend it. (Again, the Nissan.) We believed that the grandmother, in forgetting to pass along the gene for ambition and success to her son, Danny's father, had also forgotten to pass along the gene for taste, for imagination, for knowing how to spend what you have.

Of course, we got older. Mrs. Hatchet died our freshman year of high school. Danny's father was in and out of rehab, and Danny himself seemed only a few years away from the same fate. The grandmother died. The checks stopped coming. Mr. Hatchet inherited, but not as much as he had hoped. He cut Danny off. It was for his own good, he said. Time to teach him responsibility, he said. But we were in our twenties by then, just out of college, too old to be taught anything we hadn't already learned. That's when Danny started calling, asking us for money. "Don't do it," our mothers said. "Mr. Hatchet said he's only using the money to buy drugs."

"He should know," we said under our breaths.

"What's that?" they asked.

"Oh, nothing, nothing."

At first it was an us-against-them thing, and we couldn't help but give him money. Twenty here, a hundred there. Maybe each of us thought we were the only one he was asking. But eventually we married, had babies, acquired bills. The twenty here and hundred there got annoying. But that wasn't till later.

IT WAS DANNY WHO, a week after Thanksgiving, hit a dog the year we got our driver's licenses. (This was almost exactly one year after Mrs. Hatchet committed suicide, though nobody really talked about it like that.) And so leave it to him to be the downer, the precautionary tale we told each other on long, slow drives home from the movie theater or trips to the mall. "Slow down already," we might say, nearing the hairpin curve on Sycamore. "You're going to Hatchet something if you don't slow down." We were sophomores, newly sixteen, a year shy of missing Nora Lindell terribly. We were creeps, jerks, idiots. We were boys; we couldn't help ourselves.

Trey Stephens was in the passenger seat the night Danny hit the dog. They were going to a party or coming from one. Who can remember? What we remember is that Danny Hatchet hit a dog. It was late, dark. Trey said to keep driving. "Book it, man," would have been the way he said it. "Flee the scene." But already Danny was leaning towards vulnerability as his signature trait in life, towards skittishness and sensitivity. He'd only recently learned of Sarah Jeffreys' rape, though it had happened years earlier. Probably he was already feeling guilty about insisting he put his fingers where another man had violently and disrespectfully put himself.

And then, that night, there was a glint, a thud, a howl. In the headlights, to the right of the car, knocked into the grass, there was a dog, panicked, hyperventilating, not unlike Danny.

Maybe, if we'd been there, we too would have preferred to flee the scene, happy to be told what to do, to have someone else make the decision. Who knows? And maybe Danny also wanted to drive away, leave the dog, but even in the dull yellow light of the Nissan's headlights, he could see the dog wasn't dead. He could see the thing flopping around, trying to get up. Trying, but falling, whimpering. It was pathetic. The whole thing was just too pathetic. And this, more than anything, is why Danny got out of the car.

He'd seen it in a movie, probably, that you should cover an injured animal's head so it can't bite you while you're trying to save it. Because how else would Danny have known to take off his shirt and toss it on the dog's head?

"It was crazy," Trey told us the next night, while we sat or stood or crouched around Trey's basement pool table. "You should have seen it. I didn't know what the fuck he was doing." Trey told the story, of course, but Danny was there, his back to us. He stood at the sliding glass door, waiting, like any minute he might make a break for it, leave us, leave this neighborhood behind. But he stayed through the entire story, interrupting only occasionally to disagree or shake his head and say something quietly, not even defensively, like, "No, that's not how it happened."

What did happen, though, was Danny eventually got the dog in the backseat of his dad's car. Trey hadn't moved from the passenger seat, except to roll down the window and yell at him. "You're fucking crazy," he said, half laughing, half shivering in the cold. "This is fucking crazy. Ah, man, there's blood."

The dog was whimpering. Trey gave us a great impression. "Mmmm," he said, pulling up his hands in front of his chest and letting his fingers fall limp. "Mmm. Errrrr. Mmmmmm. Bambi eyes," he said, opening his eyes wide and innocent. "Fucking Bambi eyes this dog had." We laughed because it was funny—Trey moaning like a sick animal. But a glance at Danny's back and we couldn't help, one at a time, a singular private thought, to wince at Trey's delivery. We couldn't help but be thankful we weren't there, even as we said, repeatedly, things like, "Man, oh, I wish I'd been there."

The dog's back legs were mangled, sloppy, limp. There was blood all over the backseat, though neither Danny nor Trey could stop the bleeding. "Blood all over," Danny told us from his station at the sliding glass doors. The night a black wall in front of him. "That's true. Blood everywhere."

Trey asked about a tag once Danny was back in the front seat. Maybe he thought they could dump the dog with the owners and keep going, forget the accident ever happened.

"Collar. No tag," said Danny. "I checked." He wiped his face.

"Oh shit," said Trey. "You're crying? Oh shit. Too

much, man. Crying?" (And this is where Danny had said from his spot at the sliding glass doors, again softly, "No, that's wrong. No crying," though he didn't say it angrily; it was just a necessary argument to make.) Trey was laughing in the passenger seat; it would have been impossible not to laugh. Laugh or cry, your choice, but if you imagine the moment— really close your eyes and think about two boys sitting in a car by the side of the road late at night, all alone, a dying dog in their backseat—you understand that something—something guttural and uncontrollable—had to be released from the body in order just to make it through.

"Fuck you," said Danny finally. "Fuck you, fuck you."

Sitting in the front seats, the boys turned and looked at the dog. It was cold that night and Danny should have been cold without his shirt but if he was, he wasn't aware of it. He was skinny and muscle-y in that undeniably poor way. The muscles of hard times, of a body ready to fend for itself, of a body whose mother wasn't around to feed it properly. He touched the dog's ribs. It whimpered.

Trey broke the silence. "What's the plan, man? This is bad, you know. Bad. So what's the plan?"

Danny started the car. "We take him to the vet." Simple, straightforward, the right thing to do.

And that *was* the plan, and it's what Danny meant

to do. It's where Danny pointed the car when they finally started moving again. But the dog died before they'd driven a mile, and so where they ended up—some indeterminate number of hours later, past curfew if either of those two had had a curfew, which they didn't, but many hours past *our* curfew—where they ended up was in the woods, probably not too far from where the man in the Catalina might eventually take Nora Lindell. Two counties over, who knows how many miles away from us and our houses, into the forest, near the water, close to the clearing. They drove the Nissan into the woods and the dog, dead finally, was chucked by both boys onto the ground. "A missing dog is better than a dead one," Trey had said, and left it at that.

Danny would have covered the dog with leaves. Trey didn't have to say it for us to know for certain this happened. Danny didn't like things in pain; he wouldn't have liked the idea of a dead dog exposed, and so he would have covered the dog with leaves. In part out of respect for the dog, in part out of disgust for what he'd done, in part out of some twisted memory of his mother. Trey would have gotten back in the car, ready for the night to be over, the novelty of the hit having worn off for him. Maybe he would have used Danny's shirt to wipe up the blood while he waited. But the blood would have been dry by then or at least clumpy, gelatinous. If anything, he would have made the mess bigger, spread the stain farther.

THE DOG, WE FOUND out later, belonged to the Wilsons, whose kids were still in middle school. We didn't feel accountable to them, and so when the "missing" signs went up, we kept our mouths shut, managing somehow to keep this secret from our mothers. It felt like the first of any real conspiracies.

All over town, the signs were posted, signs that, unwittingly, were the precursor to Nora Lindell's "missing" signs. The reward money–$5,000–was instantly infamous; our mothers said it was disgusting. Our mothers said rewards like that were why dogs got stolen in the first place. Trey wondered aloud on more than one occasion whether the Wilsons would still fork over the money if they knew the dog was dead. We thought that was going a little too far, but only said so behind his back.

It was Nora, actually, who was the one to finally tell Trey to give it a rest. A few weeks had passed since Danny had hit the dog. Winter break would be over soon; classes would start just after New Year's. Trey had thrown an impromptu party after his parents had, last minute, gone out of town. The night was winding down. The majority of us private schoolers still had curfews, which meant the party couldn't last the way Trey wanted it to.

"Cut it out," Nora had said, loudly, unexpectedly, and seemingly out of nowhere. It's not like we hadn't noticed she was there. Of course we noticed her. Who else but Nora would have been forced to bring her little sister to a party? Who but a widowed father would be naïve enough to let his fifteen-year-old daughter take her middle school sister to a high school party? But we'd forgotten her in the way that you can forget a quiet girl. We'd forgotten her because she'd turned herself inward, willed herself invisible, at least until Trey had started picking on Danny.

The point is, Trey had one of the "missing" signs clutched in his fist and he was waving it in Danny's face, saying, "Danny or five thousand dollars? Danny or five thousand dollars?" He'd been waving the sign in Danny's face the last few weeks, since Thanksgiving, really. And, yeah, honestly, the whole thing had gotten boring. But it didn't seem our place to say. It hadn't, until Nora spoke up, seemed our place to say anything at all.

"Excuse me?" Trey said. In a movie, this would have been the moment the music screeched to a halt. But it was real life. The music, whatever it was, played on. "Did you say something?"

"I said to give it a break," said Nora. She was sitting with her back to the giant aquarium. Her cheeks were rosy. Sissy was lying on the carpet next to her, braiding her own hair into lopsided cornrows. The little sister, interesting to note, looked embarrassed, as if she didn't yet know where to side. "It's boring already," said Nora, not looking up. Not looking at anyone, especially not Trey. "No one's laughing."

For a minute we thought Danny might cry.

We waited. All of us. Our eyes on Trey. It was his house, after all. It was his right to set the tone. Danny slinked away to the bathroom. Sissy held her breath. Her mere existence, back then, was annoying. Whether she wanted to be or not, she was a chaperone. There was no telling what would remain secret when a middle schooler was among us.

"Whatever," said Trey finally, which is when the music would have miraculously turned back on. Instead, we all started breathing again, beginning to plot our blasé escapes home in time for curfew without seeming like there was a curfew to abide. Trey, of course, sounded like a jerk and we all felt embarrassed, but if any of us had been paying attention at the time, we would have noticed that the important detail was that he *did* give it a break. That the "missing" sign went not into his back pocket this time, but into the trash can finally, and we should probably have realized then— though we didn't, how could we? We were children after all—that there must have been something going on between Nora and Trey for a while.

EXCERPT FROM COURT RECORDS, CASE FILE AF7845.

DETECTIVE: Let the court records show that present in the room are Detective Rose Peters, Geraldine Epstein, and Mrs. Linda Epstein.

GERALDINE: People call me Ginger.

DET: Okay, Ginger. I'm sorry about that. Why don't we go ahead and get started, then?

GERALDINE: That doesn't mean I want you to call me Ginger.

MRS. EPSTEIN: Ginger, please. There's no reason to be rude.

DET: It's okay, Mrs. Epstein. Completely understandable. Geraldine, what would you like me to call you?

GERALDINE: I don't care. Call me Ginger.

DET: All right, Ginger. Why don't you tell me about Trey Stephens.

GERALDINE: I'm here against my will. Can you write that down? This isn't my idea.

MRS. EPSTEIN: Ginger, we talked about this.

DET: Your dissent will be noted in the court records, Ginger. And, again, we'd like to thank you for being here. We know it isn't easy or comfortable.

GERALDINE: I knew what I was doing. That's my point. I started it.

DET: I understand you feel that way. I understand that's what you think.

GERALDINE: This is what I'm talking about. Mom, this is why I don't want to be here. Nobody's listening to me. Nobody's fucking *listening* to me.

MRS. EPSTEIN: Ginger. Stop it.

GERALDINE: *You* stop it. I hate that you people think I don't know what I've done. It's not how I *feel*. It's what I *know*.

MRS. EPSTEIN: Please, Ginger. Just think about it. Think about what he's done to you.

GINGER: You're a cow. You're a fucking cow. You know that?

DET: Mrs. Epstein, maybe you could give your daughter and me some time alone?

MRS. EPSTEIN: I'm not a bad mother. I'm not a bad mother.

DET: Nobody's saying that.

GINGER: *I* am.

DET: Please, Mrs. Epstein. Outside. Let the court records show that Mrs. Epstein is no longer present.

GINGER: Amen.

DET: All right, Ginger. Let's try this again. Why don't you tell me what you *know* about Trey Stephens?

GINGER: We fucked, right? If my mom hadn't walked in on us, I wouldn't be telling you, okay? I'd probably be fucking him right now if I could. But everyone knows and so, okay, we fucked. Good?

DET: Remind me how old you are?

GINGER: So you can tell me I don't legally know what I want?

DET: Something like that.

GINGER: I'm not a child. I understand the law.

DET: Then you understand that, according to the law, you are a child?

GINGER: Do you want to know about how I fucked him? Do you want details? Like about his penis? Should I describe it so you know for sure about what I've done?

DET: Do you understand that what's happened between you and Trey Stephens has affected your childhood? Do you know that most children your age don't know about penises and *fucking*?

GINGER: First of all, I don't think that line of questioning is appropriate or very policeman-like. Second of all, that's a joke about most kids my age not knowing about penises. Hate to ruin your feel-good idea about me and my friends' childhoods, but a joke.

DET: Do you have boyfriends at school?

GINGER: Mr. Stephens is a man. Those creeps at school are boys. It's embarrassing. Seriously. The way they fiddle with you, like they're going to cry or pee their pants. It's embarrassing.

DET: All right. Let me ask you this. Do you think it's strange that *a man*, as you call him, wants to touch your body? Can you see the differences in your body and, say, my body? Can you see that there is, perhaps, something unusual in *a man* wanting to touch something so undeveloped?

GINGER: Are you trying to give me a complex? My boobs are actually pretty big, for my age. I've got the fourth largest boobs in my grade. So don't try to give me some sort of complex, okay? I get that from my mom.

DET: You miss my point, Ginger.

GINGER: Do I?

DET: All right. How about this? How about let's start with how you met Trey Stephens.

GINGER: I've known Mr. Stephens all my life. He comes to parties. We go to parties and he's there.

DET: Do you think that's strange?

GINGER: Why would it be strange?

DET: Does Mr. Stephens have children?

GINGER: So, what, he can't come to my parents' parties because he doesn't have children? Whoops. My aunt is fucked. I guess she won't be coming to any more parties because she can't have babies.

DET: Again, you miss my point.

GINGER: Again. Do I?

DET: This isn't going anywhere.

It was well after midnight and spitting rain when the Mexican left the restaurant. There was a puddle outside the back door. He skipped over it and felt foolish in the process. He was a large man, but not soft. He was barrel-shaped and strong. Far from dainty, and yet that's exactly the impression—not the word, for surely he thinks in his language and not in ours—he often has about himself. *Remilgado*, he might have said aloud. *Remilgado.* Perhaps he spit to offset the daintiness.

As was often the case, he was aware of his smell. Aware of that mixture of grease and sweat, of fried fat and meat and bleach. The rain worried him. Surely it would compound the smell of the restaurant, spread the stink evenly across his skin. He would need to shower before climbing into bed next to Nora. He dreaded waking her. Dreaded her reaction to the odors he brought home. She would not be rude; she didn't know how to be rude. She had never once said anything about the smell. But this, in many ways, was the most embarrassing thing of all. The Mexican worried that she didn't mention the smell because she believed the smell was inherent to him, believed it was a part of him, his heritage, and this was why she said nothing.

What the Mexican couldn't know was that Nora didn't simply tolerate the smell, she adored it. Late at night, the babies asleep, the high bedroom windows open, she knew when the Mexican was home first by smell, then by sound. Most nights she stayed in bed, completely still, her back to the bedroom door, and listened as he tried not to make noise. This always made her smile. She listened to the bathroom door open, to the flush of the toilet, to the sound of the shower. He took care with his laundry, never leaving it in the bedroom with the other clothes, but taking it always directly to the washing machine.

She knew he was embarrassed, but she couldn't say anything. He would misunderstand, this was certain. He would take her protestations as sympathy or guilt. Anyway, something we all know is that Nora wasn't good at speaking plainly. Maybe with strangers—with the man in the Catalina, with the woman who first hired her in Arizona, with that ridiculous stewardess in our hometown airport—perhaps with these types of people she felt emboldened, she felt free not to be herself but to be different from what she'd been trained to be. Because who, after all, knew definitively who she was? Certainly not Nora Lindell. The last to try to explain her departure from us all would be Nora. Why did she get into that car? Did she even get into it? Why did she leave our town? Why didn't she have an abortion when she could? These were questions Nora would never dare ask; they were questions, instead, that she left to us.

At any rate, one thing we knew—we know—is that Nora was not one for speaking plainly to the people she cared about. Blame her mother's death. Blame a loving but taciturn father; blame an entire town full of boys who were too shy to talk and so only stared. Blame anything you like. What we know is that Nora was one of the quiet ones. One of the inward-turned ones. Someone who was better at watching than at interacting, but whose observations served only to confuse, rather than to clarify.

And then there was Trey Stephens. How they came to be, none of us knew for sure. Silence was almost certainly part of the equation. The fish tank in Trey's basement. That faint blue light. A hand. A knee. A soundless, awkward desperation.

If she'd not been able to talk to Trey, to talk to her father, to talk to Sissy or Sarah Jeffreys or anyone from this life, then how could she have talked to the Mexican? How could she talk to anyone when she couldn't talk to us?

BUT WHEN WAS THIS, anyway? The Mexican had come home. It was raining, close to one in the morning. This was surely after they'd had sex, long after the twins had been born. But does it matter? We know they were married by this time. But does any of that matter really?

What matters is that she crept to the laundry room while he was in the shower. She crept to the laundry room and, without turning on a light, she pulled his dirty clothes from the washing machine and put them on one by one. She put on his clothes and curled up in a ball at the base of the machine. He found her asleep in his terrible, stinking clothes, and he picked her up and carried her to their bed and they faced each other while the babies slept in the room next door and they promised each other they would never leave. Nora cried and tried hard not to think of Sissy, and the Mexican held her. He said, "Let me take these clothes from you. They are dirty. They do not deserve you." By which, of course, he meant that Nora did not deserve them. She hit his chest. He let her.

"That's not what you mean," Nora said.

"I know," he said.

"Say what you mean," she said.

"I do not know how to say what I mean. You are too much," he said.

"No, no," she said. She was panicky. "Don't say that. Don't say that. I can be less."

He was silent, sad. "You misunderstand me again." She hit his chest. He grabbed her fists in one hand. "Listen," he said. "You are everything. I do not deserve you."

"But you do," she said. She tried to hit him, but his hand held hers tightly. "You do," she said again, still crying, sighing faintly.

"Your face is wet," he said. She blew her nose into his shirt that she was still wearing. He pulled the cloth away from her face.

"The babies," she said. "Who will take care of the babies?" And this is when the Mexican laughed, laughed though he was frightened by the tiny woman he held in his arms, the tiny girl he did not understand. "I will take care of the babies. I will take care of you and the babies. My babies. Three babies. All of you mine."

A breeze came in then through those high bedroom windows, a breeze that rose up from the herb garden, touching the quiet surface of the pool, picking up its faint smell of chlorine. Nora closed her eyes and breathed in heavily, taking in the scent of the eucalyptus plant, envisioning its crippled limbs and its coin-shaped leaves.

"Do you miss your sister?" she said.

The Mexican squeezed her tightly, then turned her body so that she faced away from him, and he held onto her from behind.

"Every day," he said.

"Me too," she said. "Every day."

He balled her hands into fists and grasped them tightly in his own hands. Her arms were crossed. She was locked into the position of a straitjacket. She realized this suddenly and smiled, though the Mexican could not see.

"I'm a crazy person," she said and laughed.

"*Sí,*" he said. "*Chica loca. Mi americana muy demente.* This I am sure I do not misunderstand."

Nora and Sissy missed the worst of us. Not *us*–not Danny Hatchet or Chuck Goodhue or Paul Epstein or Jack Boyd or Tommy Bowles–but the boys one year below us. (Mrs. Dinnerman would have said the boys beneath us.) Already things were changing.

But we–yes, this time *us*–had been offered the chance to show our maturity just before graduation. We'd been given the opportunity to choose a movie that we–the seniors–could watch alone in the auditorium, a kind of class date. We'd done the mature thing and invited the juniors. This pleased the school. They took it as proof that they'd taught us correctly, with dignity and class and the desire to share. We'd done the immature thing, though, and chosen *9½ Weeks*. The administration no doubt had wanted to stop it. But they were determined to stand by their choice to give us this small taste of autonomy.

THE AUDITORIUM WAS NEW that year, a double-decker affair, with a small balcony to accommodate the growth in numbers the high school was eventually hoping for. If it weren't for its newness, it might actually have been handsome. Time will tell. It was built on a bluff, overlooking the water, trees all along the steep decline towards the river. (This is the river, by the way, that we were forbidden to visit alone. An insurance nightmare, for sure. It's also the river where almost every one of us, Trey included, who didn't even go to school with us, smoked pot for the first time. It was a show of rebellion, of willpower, to defy the school and sneak to the campus-bound riverbank in small numbers. And to do this at night– to deliberately return to the place that held us captive eight hours a day–this was even more a show. But this river, remember, is also the river that runs almost the entire length of the state, that flows through six counties, including the one two over, where they not too long ago discovered human remains.)

On the night of the screening–it was late spring, humid in a chilly way, the cicadas had molted a month early, the sound of their abdomens rubbing against bark was deafening—we posted a couple seniors at each of the entrances. Drew Price and Winston Rutherford took the west entrance. (We paired the two of them because of the massive difference in their heights. At the time, it was probably as simple as thinking that Winston's six and a half feet looked funny next to Drew's five feet and change.) Paul Epstein and Jack Boyd manned the east entrance. (Jack was an athlete and a brute, which compensated for Paul's being such a pushover.) The rest of us were scattered throughout the lobby. Trey Stephens, you'll remember, was wearing camo where he hid behind the boxwoods outside the east entrance. We said he could come in only after everyone was in their seats. Somehow, allowing Trey on campus seemed more of a breech than sneaking to the river after dark to smoke pot.

At any rate, this stratagem of placing seniors at the doors as though they were guards was to guarantee that the juniors were kept in place. We'd agreed that while we felt we were generous enough to invite them to our movie, we did not feel we were magnanimous enough to invite them to sit with us. (Perhaps this had to do with James McElvoy, the junior who had already dated four senior girls and, if the rumors were true, slept with at least three of them. We saw this as trespassing. The senior girls were ours, whether they wanted us or not. We had them at least through the end of the academic year. It was only fair.)

At any rate, it was our job to ensure the juniors sat upstairs in the balcony. What's funny now, thinking back, is that the balcony seems the better location, the superior place from which to view the movie. There would have been privacy up there for us and whichever senior girls (if any) had submitted to sitting by our sides. There would have been possibilities. Perhaps. But at the time, the balcony seemed as good a place as any to corral the juniors, merely for the sake of being able to.

The juniors were surprisingly compliant, which disappointed us. We'd expected balking, especially from James McElvoy and his crew of basketball and tennis stars. But the juniors were downright polite about the whole thing. This should have been a warning. It should have, but it wasn't.

WHO KNOWS AT WHAT point they decided to do what they did? Maybe it was completely spontaneous. One of them started, and another dozen in the front row followed suit. It was probably something as simple as James McElvoy getting a hard-on accidently. It wouldn't even have been during one of the more vivid sex scenes. It would have been because of the anticipation. Mickey Rourke cutting that red pepper. Kim Basinger in those tube socks. Who of us didn't have to push down into our seats when we saw those legs, that one foot up on tiptoe, shy, innocent, and yet everything opposite those things? Her hair was wet. That's a detail every one of us remembered. It was embarrassing, watching him shell and cut the eggs. Watching what we knew or hoped was coming. It was embarrassing, which is what made it so sexy.

We don't blame his erection. We don't blame him getting hard. We blame that there, in the balcony, in the front row, James McElvoy unzipped his pants and went to town. We blame that a dozen of his friends sitting to his left and to his right, rather than stop him, followed suit. And we blame that awful moment when the thirteen of them, almost in perfect unison, stood, leaned forward, and finished in the air, their product landing on the heads of almost a dozen senior girls.

Imagine that if you can. It was awful, seeing the girls afterward. There were shrieks at first. Little high-pitched shrieks. At first we shushed them. We didn't understand. And then slowly, word went around. And we realized what had happened. We didn't believe it at first. We thought they were being dramatic, looking for attention. Then we heard the laughing, the gig-gling from above. The lights were turned on.

It was difficult to know how to react—to stay with the girls or to go for the juniors. The girls, the ones who were hit, were almost immediately placed in a protective huddle by the girls who weren't. They seemed to be taking care of themselves, of their own. Something we've never talked about since, something we all hate thinking about, is Sarah Jeffreys. She was there, in the center of the group, clearly with the girls who had been hit. This seemed the most egregious of the juniors' errors. To touch her again with something she didn't ask to have touch her, this seemed the worst of their transgressions. And yet, when the reports were finally made, when the school had been notified and the meetings had begun, Sarah's name was not among those filing complaint. We somehow knew not to say, not to insist, that she too was among them. And the girls protected her. If any of us had ever said anything (which we didn't), the girls would have denied it. They were loyal like that. Fierce. It was a loyalty and ferocity that frightened us, intrigued us, and somehow separated the sexes even more.

WHAT HAPPENED THAT NIGHT after the lights were turned on was what's been described—the girls huddling, making their exit somehow without having to leave the pack. An amorphous bundle, moving as one, out the west exit, into the parking lot, away from us.

The juniors we watched leave. They were still

laughing, James McElvoy at the lead. We watched them vacate their seats, watched them descend the stairs, watched them take the east exit to the lower parking lot. To be fair, Trey Stephens offered to take care of James himself. He said there wouldn't be the same ramifications for him that there would be for us. He couldn't get expelled for beating up a kid at a school he didn't attend. We told each other we were protecting him when we said no. We told each other we were doing the right thing. But what really must have been going through our heads, what we really must have been thinking, was that if we let Trey go after James, we'd have to follow suit. There were thirteen of them, after all. But we were cowards. We stayed in the auditorium, the movie still playing, though you couldn't really make out the images with the lights turned on full blast. Trey kicked a seat and the bottom bobbed up and down, the noise resonating in the near-empty building. There seemed nothing left to say. We were silent awhile, a few of us even took our seats, but finally Danny Hatchet said he had weed in the glove compartment of his dad's Nissan, and just like that we trekked down to the river.

For the first time, we didn't feel afraid of the river or of being caught. For the first time, we sat on the wet bank passing a joint and felt a sort of imperviousness. Whatever we had done, whatever we might do, we hadn't done and didn't do *that*. We didn't do what James McElvoy had done. And for everything in the world that existed to actually be scared about, sitting at the river smoking a joint seemed the least of it. We were growing up. It was one of those moments when you could practically feel the adult pushing out, pushing forward into the world. Perspective suddenly existed where it hadn't existed before. This was just the beginning of our lives—*our lives*, things that we were responsible for, things that we could control. It seemed all at once too big and too simple an idea.

And maybe it wasn't until then, down there next to the water, the cicadas louder than ever, that we realized exactly what had happened and the implications of it all. It wasn't until that clammy, dark silence when we realized just how truly wrong they had been.

Danny's dad could be the coolest guy in the world or he could be the weirdest. Again, take the Nissan, for example. Totally weird that he bought a brand-new 300ZX, but totally cool that he let Danny use it whenever Danny (or any of us) wanted after he turned sixteen.

If you caught him on a good day—when you were calling to get Danny to come pick you up from wherever you'd been stranded by your mom or one of your other friends—he might say something like, "Oh, hey, Buddy. I'm doing great. Real great. I'm fixing eggs for my bride, taking my dog out to pee, watching the raspberries bloom." When things were good—this was before Mrs. Hatchet died—he referred to Danny's mother as his bride.

When things were bad, he usually didn't answer the phone. But if he did answer the phone, he usually misunderstood who you were, mistaking you for an adult or one of his coworkers. Either he'd get real quiet, real sad, say things like, "Oh, Buddy, I'm not good. Not good at all. Listen, I just need a little up front," or he might answer the phone already yelling, already midway into a conversation you weren't a part of: "Not again. Not fucking again. I'm not going to tell you again."

When things were bad, we usually just hung up the phone, or wrote Danny off for the weekend, because it was just too difficult to get through to him; because staying on the phone listening to a grown man unravel was just not within our purview at the time. Instead, we'd hang up the phone and call someone else, someone like Trey Stephens, who was almost always thrilled to have an excuse to get out of the house and come get us, no matter where we were or what we were doing, the novelty of the basement bedroom having worn off a long time earlier for Trey Stephens.

THINGS FOR MR. HATCHET were almost always bad after Mrs. Hatchet died. He drank more than ever, probably he was doing drugs, too. His clothes went from simply dorky to out-of-date overnight. His breath smelled like canker sores, like horse manure and rotten fish. His hair turned gray.

All that said, we spent a strangely large amount of time with the two remaining, male Hatchets our final two years of high school. Danny's dad's place, overgrown with kudzu, was where we all smoked cigarettes for the first time. Mr. Hatchet practically lit them for us. He also bought us beer. Not even Trey Stephens' dad would do that. It was a haven during the Nora Lindell fiasco—a place we could talk openly without fear of parental interruption—especially on those nights when Trey Stephens would grow suddenly moody and kick us out of his basement.

The Hatchet door was always open to us. And we appreciated that. It was hard to *not* want to take advantage of such generosity. Mr. Hatchet's place, you'll remember, was on the short list for where to host the Halloween party the year after Nora Lindell disappeared, but the Jeffreyses won out, what with Sarah's sad situation and Mrs. Jeffreys' determination to control our comings and goings. (Probably none of the parents liked the history of suicide in the Hatchet house. Though honestly, can you imagine what an eerie, awesome Halloween party that would have been?)

Mr. Hatchet's was where we found ourselves the

night of the senior movie. It was the only place we could think to go where—stoned, drunk, rowdy, but also sullen with cowardice—we would not be immediately found out, immediately separated, questioned, and punished.

You'll remember that Mr. Hatchet was already a little punchy by the time we drove over there that night. There were no lights on upstairs, and a few of us suggested to Danny that maybe his dad was asleep and we should just call it a night. But Danny didn't even listen to us. He just plugged in the code to the garage and stood back while the door opened. The lights were off in the garage too, and it would have been impossible for each of us not to think, for at least a moment, even Danny, about his mother.

Rumors for a long time insisted that it was Danny who found her in the garage. But Paul Epstein, not too long after Danny hit the dog, got drunk on a couple sips of Wild Turkey and, out of nowhere, demanded that Danny set the story straight. Imagine that for a minute. Imagine one idiot sixteen-year-old asking another idiot but grieving sixteen-year-old to give up the goods on how his mother died and whether or not he was really there. It would be easy to blame Paul for his indiscretion, easy to ridicule him for his insensitivity. Except that most of us were just relieved that it hadn't been us to get drunk and ask, because we'd all been wondering the same thing.

There are lots of ways Danny could have responded to Paul that would have been totally legitimate, totally understandable and forgivable. He could have hit him, for one thing. That definitely would have been justifiable—almost once an hour, from the day he was born, Paul Epstein's face was begging to be hit square in the jaw. Another option might have been for Danny to cry. It would have been embarrassing as hell, but we would have understood the tears and eventually we could have forgiven them.

The option that was least forgivable, and least foreseeable (at least by us), was Danny having the nerve to paint a vivid picture. But that's exactly what happened. Who can remember the basement we were in when it happened? Trey's, maybe? Marty Metcalfe's, if it was early enough in the evening? The basement doesn't matter. What matters is that Paul asked a seriously inappropriate question and instead of anyone calling him on it, instead of any of us punching him in the nose, Danny decided to give him—to give us—more of an answer than we wanted and much more than we deserved.

To be honest, when he started talking, he seemed relieved, which makes sense. Mrs. Hatchet was dead. Mr. Hatchet was straddling the fence between occasional sobriety and full-tilt drunkenness. Our high school hadn't yet hired a counselor. (It would take another year and a missing girl for that to happen.)

So it makes sense, a little, as awful as it sounds, that Danny Hatchet might have been thankful when somebody finally asked what happened. Who else would he have been able to talk to in the meantime? No one.

"It wasn't me," was the first thing he said. "Kind of wish it had been. I don't know. I'd have liked to see her one last time alone like that. That's sick, right? I don't know. But it wasn't me."

For the first time since we'd known each other, Danny Hatchet commanded the room. Chuck Goodhue, Jack Boyd, Winston Rutherford, everyone—especially Paul Epstein—was quiet when Danny started talking.

"She was sick," he said. "Not like in the brain, like sad or anything. But with cancer. My dad knew. She was sick and she was worried about my grandma taking care of everything and I guess maybe she was worried about me." He stopped to pick a scab on his forehead. We waited for it to bleed, but it didn't. "Some days it makes sense to me, you know. Some days I can follow her fucked-up mom-logic." He picked another scab. This one sprouted a red trickle of blood. "Most days it doesn't. Most days it pretty much sucks." A few of us shot evil glances at Paul Epstein, who pretended not to notice.

Danny stuck a hand into his pants' pocket and, out of nowhere, produced a joint. "Here," he said. "Somebody light this." And somebody lit the joint and we all passed it around and somehow, just like that, Danny and his weed, and somehow even his dad, became a fixture during the remainder of our high school lives. Staying with him, being with him, was the best thank-you we could give him for taking one for the team, for guaranteeing that our mothers could never befall the same fate because circumstance wouldn't allow it, paranoia and serendipity and straight-up shameful superstition wouldn't allow more than one neighborhood mother to succumb to the same terrible fate as Danny Hatchet's mom.

AND SO, YES, THE night of the senior movie, the garage door opening slowly in front of us, the lights off, the cicadas screaming around us, it would have been impossible not to think of Mrs. Hatchet alone in that empty cavern of a room. The cold concrete all around her. The storage racks filled with Danny's abandoned athletic equipment and Mr. Hatchet's unused tools. The ignition fumes thickening in her lungs. But before any of us could grow overly solemn, a light was switched on from the inside, and at the mudroom door stood Mr. Hatchet, a fresh beer in his hand.

"Boys," he would have said. "Good. You're here. I was hoping for company."

It's likely that Mr. Hatchet was the first of all the parents to be told what had happened the night of the senior movie. Probably even before the girls decided that they should tell their mothers what had happened, we had already decided to deal Mr. Hatchet in. He was safe, after all. In some ways, no longer a parent. More one of us than one of them.

"If they touched Sarah Jeffreys, I don't know what I'm going to do," said Danny.

"You're not going to do anything, kiddo," said Mr. Hatchet. "Not your place."

We were caught off guard that Mr. Hatchet wasn't as offended as we were, wasn't as vocally adamant about how far the juniors had crossed the line. We were expecting the angry Mr. Hatchet, the one who sometimes answered the phone in a cold sweat, ready to dismember whoever was calling. But what we got was morose Mr. Hatchet. What we got was sad, disappointed, sullen Mr. Hatchet. "The things people do," he said over and over again. "The things people do to each other. It's all too much, isn't it?" He opened another beer and handed one to Danny. "It's too much for me," he said. And more than one of us will swear that he drank that next beer in one easy sip. He lifted the bottle, tilted back his head, and drank. We looked at Danny, who looked at the ceiling, and within five minutes we were standing on the curb, the garage door closing behind us, wondering what the morning would bring.

Of course Nora got pregnant again. Of course the only two times she'd ever had sex she ended up pregnant. Because if sex wasn't for pleasure, then it had to be for a cause. And babies must be her cause, like it or not. This, at least, is what she told herself.

The second pregnancy was easier than the first. She knew what to expect. She wasn't alone. The Mexican, who'd been with her during much of the first pregnancy, was with her still. And this was theirs. This strange thing growing inside Nora belonged not only to her, but also to the Mexican. It brought them closer. It brought all of them closer, in the way we hoped one day our own families would be brought closer. Nora to the Mexican, but also Nora to the girls, her daughters. The sisters.

Her face fattened. She stared at it endlessly in mirrors, and in windows strong enough to hold reflections. She blew her cheeks out at the girls. "I look like a chipmunk," she would say. "I'm hideous." The girls would giggle, blow their own cheeks out in imitation.

"You will have a little boy," said the Mexican. "I can see it in your face."

"You can see fat in my face," she said. She blew her cheeks out for him too.

"You are beautiful," he said. "More beautiful than before." He held her face in his hands, something she loved, something that made her feel tiny and slight. "You have color now. You are a woman."

She winced at the word.

"You are *my* woman," he said.

"Let me be your girl," she said. "I don't want to be a woman."

"Crazy *chica*. Crazy American *chica*. You can be anything you want as long as you are mine."

"Tell me about the baby," she said. "Say it in Spanish. Tell me about him."

The Mexican could talk for hours about the baby. He could talk like this whether Nora was in the room or not. He liked the request—the chance to make noise, to blather, without risk of being understood.

Because Nora still couldn't understand the language. Not after two years even. Perhaps at first she had tried, but ultimately she'd given up. Abandoned the language, but not the Mexican.

The girls, who would throw themselves on their backs with laughter when the Mexican spoke Spanish, understood better than their mother. "*Sí*," he said. "*Una criatura.* A little baby boy. Come," he said to Nora. "I will cook us a large dinner. Cow tongue and conch. You will love it. No, no chocolate. We do not want a dark-skinned baby. Milk for you. Milk will turn the baby whiter than you. I promise you this. But no dark foods. I insist. Eat my cow tongue and conch and he will grow fat inside you."

The baby did grow fat inside her, and the color stayed in her cheeks. She continued to feel happy, look healthy. Evenings now she drove, with the girls in the backseat, to pick up the Mexican when he was off work. She liked being alone less and less. She found the hours without the Mexican almost unbearable, even as she became more and more accustomed to the company of the girls. Nights like these, she would drive the pickup to the back of the restaurant and park next to the trash cans and the loading ramp, near the milk crates and empty cardboard boxes. And here she would wait for the Mexican to return to her.

Often she napped in the passenger seat, the girls

asleep behind her, their hands always touching, fidgeting, even in their sleep. The windows down, she would drift in and out of consciousness listening to the radio station leaking out from screens in the kitchen, playing something Mexican always, something distant and strange and foreign. The crickets were at their loudest towards the end of her pregnancy. They had taken over Arizona that year. It was a quiet, brutal backdrop to the otherwise serene feeling of those nights in the back parking lot.

Some nights she wouldn't wake up until the breeze hit her face as the car rounded the corner—the Mexican at the wheel—as they left the restaurant's parking lot. On these nights he would scold her. "Crazy American. You think nothing can hurt you. Maybe one day someone tries to steal you. What then?"

"But you've already stolen me," she would say. "How can a person be stolen twice? What are the odds?"

"Yes, you are odd."

"Not *odd*," she might have said one night, laughing at him, her hand behind his neck. "*Odds*. Like luck or chance or fortune."

Perhaps he turned melancholy then. Perhaps he scolded her, as we ourselves have wanted to scold her. "Do not speak of fortune," he might have said. "Do not speak of fortune ever. The fates do not like it. It is not yours to speak of. It is for the fates to decide."

"Old man," she might have said in response, not understanding his sudden shift towards gravity. And perhaps she might have grown panicky, except that just as quickly his mood grew light again and he laughed.

"Crazy American *chica* and her crazy old Mexican man," he said. "We are a pair, yes?"

"Oh yes," she said. "We are a pair."

He clucked at her, charmed. And once home he did as he always did on those nights when she drove to pick him up. He opened the passenger-side door and helped her to her feet. And as she did on all those nights, taking his arm and his offer to help her up, she said, "My man," then put a hand on her stomach before adding, "my men." Always she would smile. The Mexican would lift the girls from the backseat, and like this, a family, they would walk into their house and go to bed.

WHAT MIGHT HAVE HAPPENED is this: Nora Lindell died giving birth to her third baby. Just as it had been for her mother, a second pregnancy was too much for her. Pick a complication—too much blood loss, a botched C-section, a blood clot. It doesn't matter. The point is that the baby lived—a girl, not a boy—but Nora died, and the Mexican was left with three little girls. Two of them white-skinned and red-headed like their mother. The smallest of them brown-eyed and brown-bodied.

The Mexican couldn't have known—how could he? Nora had brought no pictures to Arizona, no proof of another life—but it was the youngest who looked most like Nora's own mother. And he couldn't have known how happy this would have made her, and so, instead, he was disappointed that he had corrupted Nora's line. He was sad that together they had produced not one more baby in Nora's image, but something strange and dark and foreign. He could see too much of himself in the new baby. And it was because of this, maybe, that he decided to look for the family she'd left behind. Maybe.

BECAUSE, WHAT MIGHT HAVE also happened was this: Nora Lindell gave birth, at approximately twenty-one years old, to her third child—a girl, yes, and an incredibly tan-skinned one at that—and she lived. She lived, and together she and the Mexican raised the three girls in Arizona, in the desert, teaching them to distinguish real turquoise from fake, to recognize hot peppers simply by their smell, to cut fresh aloe and apply it to their wounds, to garden and to swim and to identify the stars in the desert sky. The girls learned the Mexican's language, and they learned Nora's language. And the five of them were thick as thieves. Or, at least, the four of them—the twins and the baby and the Mexican—were thick as thieves. Because Nora was close only to the Mexican. She mothered as a bystander, as a spectator. She did what she could to please the Mexican, but beyond that, she was helpless, incapable.

The new baby, when she cried, caused Nora such crippling headaches that she often returned to bed in the afternoon. Multiple days she spent in bed—so many and so often that the Mexican had to take time away from the restaurant. Nora cried during these periods, feeling guilty that the Mexican should have to work so hard. She apologized constantly, but whenever he brought the girls in to visit—"Please," he would say, "they miss their mother"—she would turn away, crying harder, the headache sharper than ever.

BUT THEN, WHY WOULD she have stayed? Why not, then, say that she gave birth and, much as she did with us, with Sissy and with her father, she left the Mexican? Abruptly, mysteriously, unexpectedly. And, so, yes, what might also have happened is that she gave birth to her third daughter and stayed long enough only to see that the Mexican loved all the girls equally and that the four of them would be happy together, and then she left. And why not then say that it was after she left, when he was all alone and frightened of fathering them poorly, that he decided to look not for Nora but for the family she'd left behind? That he felt it was his duty, not because he didn't love those strange girl babies, but because he did. Why not say this?

Maybe she disappeared from him the same way she disappeared from us—without explanation, without warning, without anything. One day here, the next day gone. All that's left: innuendoes and guesses, half-true stories and gossip about what might have been. Maybe. But why let her break the Mexican's heart? Why not give him something she never gave us? Hasn't he earned it? Hasn't he earned more than we ever did? After all, we knew her as children. We were children, and she was a child. And what do children owe each other? But a husband? Certainly a wife owes a husband.

And so, let's imagine she was honest with the Mexican. Hard to believe that three babies could come from the body of one girl, one woman, and not have the effect at least of making that girl, that woman, more truthful with the one person she ever really loved. (If you're wondering, the answer is yes, we have considered that the only reason we want Nora Lindell to love the Mexican is because he's so different from any of us. To imagine her with someone *like* us but *not* us, that would be too much.)

She would have waited until winter to leave, waited

because she knew the snow and ice and cold would help convince her it was time to go. The pool was covered and closed for the season. The twins were talking in complete sentences, throwing in Spanish here and there. *We are aquí,* they might scream from their bedroom when the Mexican came home from work at night. *We are hambrienta. We are two hungry caninas!* Hungry wolves, he called them, when he came home and picked them up, one in each arm, and squeezed them. *My hungry wolves.*

And the littlest, the dark-skinned girl, though she was not talking, she was walking now. Walking and sometimes running. She was small, so much smaller than the twins had been when they could walk, but she was something to see. A daredevil with her body. Launching it always in any direction. She hurdled the couches. She did flips off the beds. And by the time Nora left them, the littlest could scale the molding of the interior doorways. Using her feet like hands, she could propel herself to the top of a door frame and hang. Some children can't be tamed. The acrobatics only worsened the headaches.

NORA LEFT EARLY IN the morning, before the girls were awake. It was dark in the bedroom. The winter would keep it dark for a few more hours. There was snow outside, which might have lighted up the land, lighted up the bedroom windows, but it didn't. There was no moon to reflect, only clouds above, and so the room was dark and the world outside darker still.

She put her arms around the Mexican; his back was to her. She knew he was awake when he took her forearms in his hands. "Crazy American," he said.

"Yes," she said. "That's me."

"*Chica*, why do I think you are leaving me?"

She squeezed him tighter.

"Then I am right," he said.

"I don't know why I'm leaving you," she said finally. "I don't belong here. I'm sorry."

"This sounds like what they say on the television. *It's me, not you.*" The Mexican raised his pitch when he said these words. His imitation of a woman, of a soap actress perhaps. "This sounds like a lie. Like an excuse."

She was quiet.

"Have I asked too much?" the Mexican said. "Is there something I have done? Something I can do?"

Little tears were forming at the edges of her eyes.

"You're perfect," she said. "You're perfect."

"And the girls?" he said. "What of the girls?"

"They're perfect too," she said.

"Do not make fun," he said. He was angry. "You know that is not what I mean."

"I know," she said. "Forgive me." There was silence and she held him tighter, dug her nails into his skin. "I can't take them with me," she said at last.

She felt his body relax, though his hands did not loosen. "Good," he said. "At least you are not that crazy."

Her breath was shallow, uneven.

"You won't come back to me," he said. It might have been a question. She couldn't be sure. He often forgot to inflect.

"No," she said.

He turned to face her, even though there was still no light, even though they still couldn't see each other. He put her hands on his face. It was wet.

"I understand," he said. "You don't think your old Mexican understands, but he does."

"No, no," she said. She shook her head; her entire body shook. "I don't think that."

"You must listen now," he said. She used her thumbs to wipe away the wetness on his face. "You must listen and you must promise—"

"Yes!"

"—be quiet—you must promise that you will tell me about your family before you leave." Nora was quiet. She moved one of her hands to cover his mouth, but he moved it away. "This is not something to negotiate," he said. "It is only fair to the girls that I know as much as I can."

She pushed herself into him then, nuzzling her face into his armpit. Slowly, calmly, surprisingly without reluctance, she began to talk: "The smallest one, that little animal of a girl, she looks just like my mother. The spitting image. She will be more beautiful than any of us. Even more beautiful than my sister. Have I told you about her?"

Even in our fantasies, we couldn't put our own bodies next to hers. Even here, even as we ended their marriage, we could not imagine ourselves next to Nora. Instead, it was the Mexican in those final hours to whom she told the truth. And she told the truth quietly, a whisper that not even we could hear.

And they stayed like that for another hour, maybe two, Nora talking incessantly, more than she'd ever talked in those last several years, until the first of the morning light came through the high bedroom windows and she realized the girls would wake soon.

"It's time," she said.

"If you say so," the Mexican said.

"Stay in bed," she said. "Pretend to sleep. It will be easier for me."

"Nora wants what Nora gets," he said.

"No," she said. "Nora *gets* what Nora *wants*."

"Ah," he said. "Of course."

She pulled the blanket up over his shoulders. She put her hands on his eyes, now dry. "Go to sleep," she said. And the Mexican did go to sleep, and when he woke, another hour later, Nora was gone.

It is too much to imagine anything different.

She was in Mumbai for the bombings. She was on television—wasn't she?—in the background, behind the news anchor from our hometown, the one who had, amazingly, made it to prime time. It's a wonder the anchor didn't recognize her, though understandable given that strange and humid city in ragtags all around her. But what a story that would have been—to see Nora, to bring her home, to finally solve the mystery that's been nagging us all these years.

We all turned thirty the year of the bombings, which means Nora did too, or at least she would have. Stu Zblowski said he saw her on the television screen, a thirty-year-old version of the sixteen-year-old who'd disappeared. Marty Metcalfe said he saw her too. (Marty was watching because he was in love with the news anchor. She'd been at a New Year's party his parents had thrown when Marty was only seventeen. She'd gotten drunk, made an error in judgment that she swore to Marty would never happen again, and Marty had been in love ever since. It's like that sometimes.) Stu called his mom to tell her what he'd seen, but Marty was too distracted by the news anchor and the danger he believed she was in to remember to call home.

Just a month after the bombings, at someone's Christmas party (the Rutherfords? the Boyds? It was the party with the tree that had been decorated with red chili pepper–shaped lights instead of tiny white bulbs), we questioned Stu about what he'd seen. (Marty, though he was there, often proved useless when pressed for information, as if the only thing on his mind at any given minute was the news anchor and the coat closet at his parents' house and the taste of Chablis on that older, wetter tongue. Not surprisingly, Marty–like Trey Stephens and Danny Hatchet– never married. All three of them carrying the strange, unfair burdens of childhood through their entire adult lives.)

"Was it definitely her? Or was it just possibly her?" A few of us ushered Stu into the basement, away from our wives and mothers, where we could be as openly curious about Nora as we wanted.

"Clear as day," said Stu. "It was her, definitely." Stu was in town only for the holidays. He'd moved to New England, as promised, when Bethany got pregnant. And Bethany, just as *she'd* promised, gave him a new yellow Lab that readily answered to the name Stu.

Danny Hatchet scratched at his thighs, then produced a joint from a back pocket. The rest of us shook our heads like we were disappointed, or like of course Danny would have a joint in his pocket and shouldn't he just grow up already? But when he offered it around the room, every one of us accepted. A few of us perhaps shooting quick glances towards the stairway and the door at the top, making sure it was closed, making sure we wouldn't be caught, though we were adults and these were our lives and our decisions and who, really, was left to scold us in any truly meaningful way?

"What the fuck would she be doing in Mumbai?" Drew Price still dropped f-bombs like they were articles, a way of making up for being almost a foot shorter than the rest of us.

"What if she's been alive all this time and then died in the bombings?" said Chuck Goodhue. "Like the minute we almost found her, she went and died all over again, only this time for real."

"Yeah. What if? Don't be an idiot." It was Paul Epstein talking, strangely aggressive for someone who'd been reticent about Nora after that year of calling Sissy a slut—a year that most of us agree caused her to leave us in favor of boarding school almost a decade and a half ago.

"How am I an idiot?" It was Chuck Goodhue talking.

"You really want me to explain it to you?" Paul took the joint from Danny and we all watched the way he inhaled without a pause and it was the first time, probably, that any of us accepted that he was a man now, that in spite of all his literal and metaphorical shortcomings, he was, after all, one of us too.

"Fuck you, Paul."

"Fuck you, Chuck." Most of us were laughing by this point. We didn't mean to, but we couldn't control it. "Say hi to your wife for me."

"What's that supposed to mean?" It wasn't Chuck who asked the question. It was someone else. Danny? Jack? Who can remember? But it was Chuck who told us to let it go. And it was Chuck who was first to walk up the staircase to leave the party. We tried to watch him leave, tried to give his exit the respect it deserved, but our minds got away from us.

"I'm thirty years old," Winston was saying, "and Maggie's a month away from a baby and I've got a great mortgage and a great lease on a car, but Nora's in Mumbai with bombs going off and I'm fucking jealous. Someone explain that to me."

But we couldn't. We sipped our beers and shut our mouths. And while we waited out the final hour of the Christmas party—milling about the living room upstairs, hoping for our wives to tell us it was time to go—we wondered one by one, the thoughts perhaps overlapping, about not just the *possibility* of Nora in Mumbai, but the *plausibility*. Because, if she had been there since she'd gone missing, how'd she get there? Where did she get the money? From the man in the Catalina? Had she been there all this time? Did she steal it? When, and from whom? And what about a passport? What about any of the logistics? None of it made sense. All of it was unlikely. And yet. Stu Zblowski. Marty Metcalfe. They were so sure. It was impossible to ignore at least the chance that it was true.

ASK ANY ONE OF us and we'll tell you that the liquor went down easily the last hour of that year's holiday party. High from Danny's stale weed, agitated by the new information (even misinformation) about Nora, we found ourselves gulping what was meant to be sipped. Every time we glanced at our wives and were given the gentle but unmistakable shake of the head that *no*, it was *not* yet time to leave, we found our way to the makeshift bar in the kitchen, pouring whatever the guest before us had left out—eggnog, hot rum toddy, straight warm gin—into our tumblers.

In spite of that, in spite of our too-ready gullets and our lubed-up heads, there were certain other details about that party that have stayed with us. Details, surprisingly, that had nothing to do with Nora. And not just details like the fact that the chili pepper–shaped lights gave off an eerie pink glow (Was it the Rutherfords? Were they that tacky already? Or were they being ironic? Surely someone must remember at whose house this all took place?), but details, for instance, like the fact that Trey Stephens was there. We were still ten years away from the things he'd do with Paul Epstein's daughter, then only three years old. But it's the sort of thing one remembers later, when the crime is finally committed, when the past is recounted, reviewed, reevaluated, and sometimes even revised. As in, *That party? Jesus. Wasn't Trey Stephens at that party? Can you imagine? Jesus. If only we'd known.* And perhaps that, more than anything, was the refrain that was and should be reserved for Trey. *If only we'd known.* But we didn't know. We never know. No matter how many times we revisit that party or any other. The fact is, until it happened, until Trey changed how we viewed him, how we viewed and view ourselves— as men, as fathers, as friends and husbands—we could looked like a tear and when his wife turned red and walked away, we all understood what must have happened. And in case we hadn't put it together then, we definitely put it together a few hours later, in Paul's basement, where we held a wake of our own in honor of Minka, not having been invited to the family-only event being held at the Dinnerman house, hosted no doubt by that now older, still gorgeous Russian beauty, Mrs. Dinnerman.

In Paul's basement, safely out of earshot of Chuck or his wife (because of course they didn't come; they were already too busy trying to repair the injuries of a five-year infidelity), Paul told us what he'd seen.

"So it's been going on that long," said Winston Rutherford. "I figured it out last year, but Chuck said it was a one-time thing." And for some reason this turned the wake even more morose than Minka's death itself. As if the realization that there's so much that we didn't—that we don't—know that it's frightening, that it's distancing and isolating and sad.

BUT WE WERE FIVE years from that specific isolation, and back at the Christmas party with the chili pepper–shaped lights and the weirdly oily hors d'oeuvres, we found ourselves milling about the basement and then milling about the living room. We were thinking about Nora Lindell, every one of us convinced we were the only one, and the thought all the more tender because of it. We were thinking about Mumbai and all those people and the noise and the heat and the smell, and we were imagining ourselves there in it. We were imagining our own café table, our own chai tea and straw, our own glimpse of Nora, safe, alive, alone. We could feel the sweat forming on our upper lips. We could hear the screaming, the dull, directionless moaning of people scrambling for cover. We could feel the explosions, the thud of fear in our hearts. My god, yes, we could see Mumbai clear as day, a city in smoke, a city in ruins.

Maybe, in Mumbai, Nora Lindell danced. She drank, too, maybe. She wore saris and bracelets and sandals. And when she danced or drank or danced *and* drank, the bracelets jangled together the entire length of her arms. Perhaps she called herself Trinka, a name that was meaningless, that she'd pulled from the air, like it had always been there, waiting to be taken. She'd gained weight since Arizona, if Arizona had existed at all. The point is, she'd gained weight since us, since high school. She'd grown taller, wider, more feminine. The breasts she'd never wanted had also grown. And, in spite of herself, she admired them. She wore clothes to complement them, to complement the fact that she was—whether or not she liked it–a woman. Thin-strapped dresses and weightless T-shirts. Somehow, her gender didn't matter in India. She was something other than a woman in India. She was an outsider. She was a foreigner. She could do anything she wanted, and the attention, when she danced, was exhilarating.

Who knows how she got there or how long she'd been there before the bombings? Maybe she had gotten there by way of Arizona and a couple of babies. Maybe by way of the man in the Catalina. Maybe she'd been there since the year she went missing, or maybe she arrived only a few months before the bombings. Who knows?

What matters is that when she got to Mumbai she would have started drinking, taken up dancing, begun wearing dresses that were loose and tight at the same time, that hugged her body even as her body was finally allowed to move freely. And somewhere in the middle of all of it, somewhere in the dancing and the drinking and the sheer enjoyment of life as it is meant to be lived, Nora Lindell would have fallen in love. She would have fallen in love with a woman. Why? Simple. Because we are men. And so let us say that she fell for a woman. A henna tattoo artist who worked in a small room across from the hotel where Nora stayed.

"American," the tattoo artist said one day. "American. Come here."

Nora crossed the street. It never would have occurred to her that she shouldn't.

"Are you teasing me with your body?" asked the tattoo artist. "Every day you walk by me and every day I am thinking you are teasing me."

Nora shook her head.

"You have no answer," said the woman. "Then I am right."

Nora shook her head again, perhaps she even laughed a little, charmed. A faint blush spread across her chest.

"You are older the nearer you come, yes?"

"I am not a child, if that's what you mean," said Nora. It was the first thing she had ever said to the woman. She would remember it always. *I am not a child.* Why had she said it? Hadn't she wanted nothing more than to remain a child? Sitting in that Catalina, her future so unknown, hadn't she wished to be stripped of sex, to be stripped of experience, of skin, of anything carnal? Hadn't she wanted, even more, to become something genderless, something impossible and alien and innocent all at once? That girl was so far from her now. That childhood so much a thing of the past.

The tattoo artist laughed. "No, you are not a child. With that body, you could never be a child. You were born a woman, I think. Born into that body to tease me."

Again Nora blushed. But probably, in spite of the flattery, she was annoyed. She was annoyed because she didn't understand what the tattoo artist wanted or why she'd been called across the street. She was annoyed because she hadn't realized, until the tattoo artist started speaking, that she was lonely. That she had been missing, for a very long time now, the simple act of verbal communication. And she was annoyed because she might have continued on just a little longer without making this realization, without the weight of loneliness suddenly upon her.

THE ATTRACTION WAS FAST, complicated, inexplicable. It must have been the tattoo artist who made the first move because Nora wouldn't have known how—man or woman, she wouldn't have known how.

The artist's name was Abja. Abja Safia—"because I was born in water and my father would have me be chaste, which I am not," she told Nora on the night they first met, lying on the floor, their backs against pillows, "because every name must mean something. Everything has meaning. You understand this. Yes?"

"Yes," said Nora.

"Good, then you will stop calling yourself Trinka. It has no meaning."

The tattoo artist was dangerous in her intensity, which was probably what attracted Nora to her.

NORA COULDN'T REMEMBER HOW she got home that night. What she could remember was waking up, in the middle of the night, to the noises on the street. She had sweated, and under the breeze of the ceiling fan she shivered. She tried to remember her day, which she was able to do only in flashes. A sunrise. Trash. Banana peels and dark-skinned children. A glass of beer. Her feet. Her dirty toes. A woman. More glasses of beer. Pillows. Her own arms. Breasts.

She shivered again. The memories were neither real nor not real. They were neither fond nor not fond. They were, however, a catalyst for the acid in her stomach to rise, to grab hold. She clutched at her gut and turned on her side. She was too tired, too lazy to move to the bathroom. Her body heaved. Nothing came. She pulled the blanket up around her shoulders and grabbed her knees. If the man in the Catalina had ever existed, if that night so long ago in the woods, in the clearing, in the snow, under the leaves, had ever really happened, then surely Nora would have remembered that night at just this moment, just as we can't help but remember it. She would have remembered the fear, the cold. She would have remembered the way her body folded into itself for warmth, the way she shoved her knees into her chest and clutched at her elbows, reducing her surface area.

But that's only if the Catalina existed. If not,

inside. Her body heaved and the tears kept coming and, eventually, she slept.

In the morning she walked across the street to the tattoo artist's room, where she undressed and allowed the tattoo artist to change the color of her skin.

Mr. Lindell died. It's perverse of course, but we were giddy with the news that the funeral would be in our town and not in the desert, in Arizona, where he died. The obituary was a thing of beauty. The kind of thing that receives attention that the deceased never received while living. We read it, then we read it again. We studied it. We looked for signs. We picked up the phone, we put the receiver back in its cradle. We looked for indications of ourselves in it, acknowledgments that we, too, had been part of his life.

On Friday evening, June 16, at home and surrounded by his family, Herbert Hugh Lindell, age 67, quietly lost his year-long battle with pancreatic cancer. Born in Brunswick, Georgia, raised in Atlanta, Herbert lived with his daughter, Sissy, in Arizona, where he peacefully died.

Though never one to seek out compliments or gestures of praise, I think he would not object to my relating that he was a stalwart and loyal friend, a true connoisseur of ethnic foods, a word savant, an honest lawyer, objective arbitrator, geopolitical maven, and splendid husband and father.

In the words of his grandchildren, he was an all-right dude, a man among men. He will be sorely missed by his daughter, by his sister Nancy of Marietta, Ga., and by his many and adoring grandchildren.

An open ceremony will be held in Herbert's honor, as requested, in the mid-Atlantic.

The sudden, unexpected use of the first-person haunted us. The obituary was Sissy's handiwork; there was no doubt about that. And her simple use of the word *I* brought her voice, her body, her sheer strange existence back to us completely. But what caught us, what held us, what truly, truly disturbed us, was the inexplicable and undeniable absence of Nora Lindell from her father's obituary.

Sitting at our various kitchen tables that Sunday morning—our wives washing the baby in the sink or peeling potatoes for the dinner they'd been planning or sleeping in above us for the first time all week—we reread the obituary that had made its way from Arizona and wondered (even if only for a half second) whether we'd dreamed Nora Lindell into existence.

It was our mothers who broke the spell. One telephone number at a time, the phone tree was resurrected. Mrs. Zblowski called Mrs. Boyd, who called Mrs. Epstein. And our mothers, in turn, called us, dutiful as ever to the prescription of the passage of information.

"Did you see?" they asked.

"See what?" we might have said, determined as ever to feign indifference.

"The paper," they said, impatient and unbelieving, the click of their nails audible as they struck one by one on their own kitchen tables. "Mr. Lindell."

"Oh, that," we might have said, our wives furrowing their brows, wondering the reason for that Sunday's particular interruption. Perhaps we rolled our eyes at them or shook our heads. Perhaps we made chatty hands at them, suggesting our mothers' unwillingness to stop talking. Perhaps, but what we did not do was let on, was let slip, let show our absolute concentration on that obituary, its content, and whatever new information our mothers might have called to divulge.

Our backs turned now towards our wives, we moved away from them, towards the foyer or the den or the basement even, and continued our conversation. "I saw it, sure, but I haven't had a chance to read it," we might have offered. "Did it say what he died of?"

"Does it matter?" they said, their age so much more present to them, so much more real. "Are you telling me you didn't notice that they left Nora completely out of it? Left her out of it like she never even lived? It's a shame is what it is. And bad form."

"I suppose now you aren't so keen on moving to Arizona."

"I never said anything about Arizona. Who wants to live in Arizona?" our mothers said.

"Will you go to the funeral?" we said, our heartbeats racing themselves, each beat trying to surpass the one before it.

"Well, it would be wrong to slight Mr. Lindell just because Sissy slighted Nora, wouldn't it?"

"Maybe it wasn't Sissy. Maybe it was the paper," we said. "Maybe it was one of those form obituaries."

"Ha!" they said, indignant as ever, then hung up the phone to begin work on their own obituaries, page-long affairs that left nothing out, got everything straight. Children in general couldn't be counted on, and we specifically had no doubt failed them completely.

But one by one they called us back, quieter now perhaps, the recounting of their own lives having softened the vitriol: "Pick me up at ten. It's rude to be late to a funeral."

OF COURSE WE ATTENDED. How could we not? We urged our mothers towards the front rows of the church, but they demurred, insisting on sitting in the back, with their friends, out of the way of the family. One by one they broke away from us and we were left with each other, too timid now without the excuse of our mothers to make our way forward. We crowded together in the rear of the church, on the side opposite our mothers. We were a strange-looking group of thirty-three-year-old men—strange because we seemed more like children, like boys in suits for the first time. We'd forgotten our manners. (Mrs. Dinnerman would have said we'd forgotten our mannerisms.) We'd also forgotten our posture, forgotten everything our mothers had been teaching us for years. Someone picked his nose—Danny Hatchet? Another snorted—was that Paul Epstein? Who can remember? But probably it was Paul Epstein. He was always somewhat crass.

He couldn't help it; the nerves brought it out of him. Put him in a room with the principal and he'd burp uncontrollably. It was always misunderstood. Misunderstood for deliberate rudeness instead of unavoidable anxiousness.

Drew Price leaned over and whispered, "Is that 'Pancho and Lefty' they're playing? I swear the organist is playing 'Pancho and Lefty.'" We ignored him, though we'd been wondering the same thing. His insistence, though, seemed proof enough that we were wrong. When had Drew Price been right about anything—the driver of the Catalina, the true identity of his birth father? When?

Winston Rutherford was the one who first noticed the two redheads in the front row. "Holy shit," he said. "Holy fucking shit. It's them. It's Nora's daughters." If Jack Boyd had been at the funeral, he might have been able to confirm or deny whether these were the girls he'd seen at the airport in Phoenix, but he wasn't there. We were on our own to decide.

Sissy emerged from a side room before we could argue with Winston's assessment of the situation. She was dressed in black—black slacks, black turtleneck, black gloves. At her side was another girl, this one tiny and tan and without a brilliant mess of red hair. Sissy was everything we expected her to be—tall, slim, regal. Maternal and yet nothing like our mothers, nothing like the wives with whom we'd had and were having children of our own.

When they sat, it was a spectacle. Not just because they were the bereaved, but because of the way they were lined up, from biggest to smallest–just the backs of them visible, three redheads starting with Sissy, ending with the fourth, with that strange, small brunette girl. The whole lot of them cried, carried on in that way that only young girls can carry on. They wrung their hands. They held each other. They leaned into each other's shoulders and howled delicately, wetly.

Sissy, on the other hand, was reserved. Occasionally she put her arm around the one sitting closest, or leaned forward to touch the knee of the small girl sitting a few places away. But mostly she sat straight, looked forward, and waited.

AT SOME POINT SOMEONE noticed the large Mexican man sitting at the far end of Sissy's pew. He was closer to our mothers' age than to ours. He did not cry, though he appeared uneasy. Once or twice he made eye contact with us and immediately looked away. Mostly he kept his eyes trained on the girls in his row, the girls sitting next to Sissy. It seemed he'd taken a spot both close to and far from them, as if he needed the distance in order to protect them. He looked occasionally at the doors behind us, as though hoping someone might enter.

Winston Rutherford said it was obviously the smallest girl's father. We laughed at him.

"Yeah, but who's the mother? Nora or Sissy?" we asked.

"Don't be stupid," he said. "She looks just like Sissy, but with a hint of South of the Border thrown in." We took another look at the strange little girl with coloring all her own. Then we looked at Sissy. Then we looked at the Mexican.

"Sissy would have sex with that guy?" we said. "He's twice her age."

"She had sex with Danny, didn't she?" Winston said. We looked away, unimpressed. "The backseat of your dad's Nissan, right, Danny?"

Danny said, "Fuck you," under his breath. Then added, as if not sure where the true insult lay, "It's *my* Nissan now, dipshit." Someone's mother coughed from the aisle across the way.

"Anyway, that was—what?—eight years ago? Christmas, Thanksgiving?" said Paul Epstein. "Danny wouldn't have a shot at her now."

"Fuck you, Epstein," said Danny. "You couldn't even get her in high school."

"Eight years," said Epstein. "How old do you think that little one up there is?"

"I said shut up," said Danny.

Tommy Bowles, always somewhat apologetic, probably as a result of the rumors about his brother and Sarah Jeffreys and the backseat of that Dodge he refused to drive, said, "It's a funeral, guys. Give it a rest." And for a moment we remembered ourselves and our ages and our wives and our own children to whom we would go home afterwards and try to set examples for.

THE MEXICAN'S NAME WAS Mundo. "The world," he said, and sculpted his hands around an imaginary planet. "That is me," he said with a smile. He was a short man, but large, like a barrel.

We all shook his hand. He could have lifted any one of us clear off the ground. We were standing in the parking lot, reluctant to go home, reluctant to leave without talking to Sissy, reluctant to relieve our wives from the chore of babysitting.

"You knew Mr. Lindell?" asked Drew Price. Sometimes you just wanted to punch Drew, he could be so daft.

The Mexican ignored him. It's possible he didn't hear him correctly. "Sissy wants what Sissy gets," he said. "And so I am here. And because Herbert was a very good man." We nodded, not knowing where to go with the conversation.

"You've met Mundo, then," Sissy said. She'd sneaked up on us somehow. We'd all been waiting for the moment when she would acknowledge us, but we were completely unprepared when she finally did. "We wouldn't have made it this last year without Mundo. More of a nurse than any one of those idiot hospice workers. A confessional of a man. I swear, just looking at him makes me feel like I'm being hugged." She said these things to Mundo, not to us. It felt like we were spying. Still, we didn't look away.

Mundo smiled. "Confessional. I do not know about this." He winked at Sissy. "But the cook, the gardener, the caretaker," he said quietly. "Whatever you want. That is me. The world at my fingers." Again he shaped an imaginary planet with his hands. Sissy held out hers and he kissed them. Then he took her face in his giant's hands and kissed her forehead. We watched. It seemed not right that we were there, that they were doing this in front of us. Danny Hatchet blushed. Mundo lowered his head and shuffled away in the direction of those three little girls. "He was very fond of my father," said Sissy. "They played chess. Well, checkers, but my father insisted it was chess. I think he worried we wouldn't respect him–Mundo or my father–if we knew they were playing checkers. But we've all grown very attached. We don't go any-where without him anymore."

She watched us watch him. She watched us watch the girls around him. We'd been reduced to our seventh-grade selves. Unable to speak. Waiting to be called upon. Teased. Anything. Waiting for the girl to talk to us.

"The biggest—that one in the purple dress, who obviously matches the one with the ponytail, though they're not identical—is Lucy, after my mom." We nodded. It was like a scene from *The Sound of Music*, only this was a comedy or a satire, though which we couldn't tell. Sissy was deadpan, and yet it seemed she was mocking us even as she introduced the children.

"Lucy's twin is Ivy. Family names. Try not to wince, Paul, it's not polite." It would have been impossible not to wonder just then, if only for a moment, whether or not Sissy was remembering the terrible name Paul called her that one year of high school, after her publicized tryst with Kevin Thorpe in the Jeffreys' mudroom.

We watched the girls as Sissy spoke, unwilling to look at her directly, frightened to memorize her face too perfectly, though more likely simply unwilling to have our fantasies disagreed with, repudiated. The girls, in turn, ignored us. They were focused more now on each other and their dresses. One of the twins straightened the hem of the smaller one. That one, in turn, brushed off an eyelash from the other twin's cheeks. They were not unlike monkeys or a pack of wild ponies. They seemed completely foreign, completely different from the tamed children we had at home.

"The brunette is called Nora," Sissy said, regaining our attention, though not our eye contact. For a moment we looked at the tiny, tan Nora in front of us, the one least like the Nora we had known. One by one, perhaps mere seconds apart, we looked at the swarthy-skinned Danny Hatchet and again remembered his story of the pool hall and tequila and his father's Nissan (his now!) with Sissy Lindell in the backseat. We tried the math in our heads, convinced one minute that it was possible, convinced the next that it wasn't. Eight years. Was she too old to be the outcome of their brief liaison? It was too hard to tell. Her size was misleading. But to ask Danny was unthinkable, especially at a funeral. This much of our mothers' influence managed to stay with us that day.

"How long are you in town?" It was Winston Rutherford who'd managed to come up with a complete sentence.

"Outcome unclear," said Ivy, one of the twins—perhaps on the cusp of adolescence, perhaps barely pre-pubescent—who'd suddenly taken up protective residence at Sissy's side. Sissy put her arm around the girl in a tight sort of way, as if to silence and not to comfort.

"Remains to be seen," said Sissy. "I'll probably be at that bar on High Street later tonight, though. My aunt's agreed to watch the girls. Spread the word, if you want. Company will definitely be appreciated."

OUR WIVES WERE STRANGELY compliant when we told them about Sissy and her unexpected invitation to have drinks at the bar on High Street the night of her dad's funeral. We thought, at first, that they had misunderstood us—that we were inviting them to go with us—and we panicked. They seemed amused by our confusion, which made us feel young, made us feel like children, and we didn't like it. Somehow, the older we got, the less we were taken seriously by the women in our lives—mothers, wives, and one day soon, even our daughters.

"Don't worry," they said, bouncing the baby up and down, hoping to get the last of the hiccups out of those tiny lungs. "I know I'm not invited. It's fine. We'll take the dog for a walk, watch a movie. Really, it's fine." They rubbed our backs and laughed. "You need to relax," they said. "Really. You're too young to look so anxious." The back rub felt good but also patronizing, and we worried at the implications of such a combination of feelings.

. . .

BY EIGHT O'CLOCK, MOST of us were at the bar–Paul Epstein, Jack Boyd, Winston Rutherford, Chuck Goodhue, Stu Zblowski, Drew Price, Marty Metcalfe, Trey Stephens, even Danny Hatchet, especially Danny Hatchet. We were all there. Drew and Paul were playing pool; the rest of us had taken seats at the bar. Danny ordered a round of tequila shots, and a few of us were wondering who was going to end up paying for those shots when Trey announced that the entire night was on him. It was one of those gestures we both admired and hated him for. On the one hand, the tab was taken care of and that was a relief; on the other, suddenly we were schmoes for not being able to make the offer ourselves.

We were like kids in a record store with our first summer paycheck, anxious to spend the money, desperate to find the right albums. For the first time in our lives, we didn't talk about Nora Lindell; we didn't talk about those three little girls or even the giant Mexican. Trey talked about putting a swimming pool in his backyard (his recent inheritance was clearly burning a hole in his pocket), but Jack Boyd, who'd missed the funeral but taken a cab straight from the airport to the bar and who'd chosen real estate as his calling, advised against it. "Swimming pools are money-suckers. Unless you plan to die in that house, I'd leave the swimming pool idea alone," said Jack. "Anyway, you're not married. It's not like you've got kids you need to entertain. Unless, hell, you want to build that pool and babysit for us during the summer?" We laughed when Jack said this, like it was the craziest idea we'd ever heard. Who, after all, would ever volunteer to watch a kid that wasn't his own? Trey laughed too. Of course he did. Why wouldn't he?

The thing we wonder about now—turning on the grill in the backyard, getting the coals ready and the steaks marinated—is whether or not Trey knew his inclinations even then. Was it already in him? Or did it take seeing Ginger Epstein to draw it out of him? Were there others we didn't know about, would never know about? Often it would take a wife's hand on the shoulder to pull us away from these reveries. "Honey," she might say, "the coals. Are they ready? The kids are hungry." And they would always be tender at these moments, always impossibly understanding, as though they could see our thoughts, read our fears, our worries. Sometimes, it's like they almost understand how incredibly overwhelming it all is—to be a man, to be a father, a husband, a human being, responsible for the lives of others.

WHO KNOWS HOW MANY hours we waited at that bar? How many games Paul and Drew played and lost or played and won? What we know is it was late, we were drunk, when the bartender held up the phone and said, "Is there a Daniel Hatcher here? Daniel Hatcher?"

"Hatchet," someone said.

"Is someone going to take this?" the bartender said.

Danny moved in the direction of the phone. We tried not to watch him, tried not to care who was calling or why. We probably even looked at the TV for the first time, probably asked the bartender to turn up the volume on a game we didn't even care about— all this in an effort to look like we didn't care, to let Danny, each other, ourselves, know how much we didn't care about that phone call.

Drew Price would swear later that he saw Danny slam his fist into the bar just after he hung up the receiver. Sometimes—not always—but sometimes Drew's pleasure in other people's pain was just a little too much.

"She's not coming," said Danny when he turned to face us. "Sissy. Something about the girls. But she's not coming."

Chuck Goodhue said, "Shit. Figures. I got to go," and left the bar without saying goodbye. We thought maybe it was something at home, something with Peg and the girls, and we made mental notes to call in the morning and make sure everything was all right.

When we did finally call the next day—not in the morning, it had taken us till mid-afternoon to recall his sudden exit from the bar—he was completely calm. He might even have chuckled at the earnestness with which we'd asked if he was okay. "Fine, really. You're a good man for calling. Everything's fine." Of course, we know now that night at the bar waiting for Sissy must have significantly cut into the few hours a week he was able to spend with Minka Dinnerman. "Fuck," we remember him saying as he left the bar. "Fuck, fuck."

Danny left his Nissan at the bar and Trey, after giving the bartender his credit card number and telling him to take good care of us, drove Danny home. The rest of us stayed till closing, drunk enough to reason that staying out till two a.m. would get us into less trouble than going home at midnight, drunk enough to think we wouldn't mind the ramifications in the morning.

At some point, we had started throwing pool parties of our own. "It's too much," we told our mothers, "to ask you to entertain our friends *and* their children. Come to our house," we said. "It will be easier all around." They acquiesced, though they knew what this meant. This meant we were finally in our primes, finally adults, finally able to take care of ourselves and our families. Which meant they were getting older, turning a corner, admitting defeat. But this was life, after all; this was progress; this was what we'd been born to do.

We owned homes, had wives. Some of us had more than one child by then. In many ways, we were kings. Everything was ahead of us. Exercise was voluntary, not mandatory. Our bodies promised to stay thin, retain muscle indefinitely. Our wives, though they were turning maternal, still doted on us. Still made us feel like high schoolers after they put the baby down late at night, then slipped into bed and whispered what we wanted, what we needed to hear.

DREW PRICE AND HIS wife had the biggest pool and the best outdoor barbeque setup and so it made sense, when they were willing, to have the pool parties at their place. Saturdays were ideal. Our wives were less strict about how much we drank and the kids still had a day to recover and lounge around the house, doing homework if there was any still to be done for school or camp or whatever. And it was a Saturday—we were twenty-nine that year—when the Prices threw the last pool party of the summer, the pool party that would mark the beginning of Chuck Goodhue's affair with Minka Dinnerman.

Everyone was there—the Zblowskis; Paul Epstein and his wife and their little girl; Jack Boyd (with wife number one, who lasted only long enough to have a baby and secure some pretty serious alimony); Chuck and his then-fiancée Peg Whitney; Trey Stephens with one of the nurses from Peg and Chuck's newly minted psychiatric practice; Minka (whose position at Dinnerman Mercedes meant she pulled up to every pool party in the most current luxury sedan, something we noticed our wives noticing every time); even Danny Hatchet, whose unpredictable construction schedule meant he wasn't always around, was there for a little bit of the party. And, of course, our parents were there for that party, too. They came early, had a few gin and tonics, and left just after the sun went down, just as our children started to complain about going to bed, about not getting more ice cream, about getting in the pool one last time. Complaining children always seemed our parents' cue to leave. "We've done this before," they'd say, not even attempting to make excuses or apologies as they moved towards the driveway and their cars. "We're too old to listen to babies howl. It's your turn."

AT SOME POINT, AFTER our parents left, a few of us slipped inside to switch from beer to something stronger. Though our parents drank gin and tonics at noon, it still felt strange to drink liquor in front of them. Funny that even as we were so high on life, so fully in control, we still deferred to their status as our former leaders. Senility would strip them of that title altogether soon enough. But for a while still, even as we sensed the shift, even as we felt our flow, their ebb, we still respected the memory of their youths. It's as if, somewhere far back, we were cognizant of the fact that the ebb would one day come for us—one day—but not then, definitely not then. Because, just then, we were sneaking inside, drunk already from the sun, ready to get drunker still off the strong stuff, the good stuff.

But really, those were the days: going home with our families, the bedroom windows opened high; the breeze coming in, lifting the smell of chlorine off the pool; the faint whiff of linden from the trees we'd only just planted around the pool; the babies humming in the adjacent room; our wives moving their bodies steadily over us, beneath us, their hands still deft, still young, still willing. What didn't we have then? What could we possibly have fantasized about other than what was in our hands, in our homes? Forget Nora Lindell. No, never fully forget Nora Lindell. But, for a moment, pretend that she is still with us, has always been with us. Isn't what we have still good? Isn't this life still perfectly adequate? Would she really have provided us anything our wives haven't? Perhaps. Yes, perhaps. But that night, after the Prices' last pool party of the summer, everything felt wonderful; we were whole, complete, content. We had drunk like fish, we had tanned like hides, and now we were ready to sleep like kings. Summer was almost over and we were, I do believe this, happy that night, happy that year.

"This sky could be an Arizona sky," said Nora.

"What does that mean?" asked Abja.

"Arizona? It's a state in America," said Nora. "Home of the Grand Canyon, skiing, deserts, cacti. There are mountain lions there. Did you know that? 'Good oak,' that's what the name means. *Aritz Ona.* You probably like that, because it has a meaning. The state bird is a phoenix. No. That doesn't make sense. The state capital is Phoenix. I don't know what the state bird is. I could make one up. A cardinal, maybe. Like the football team."

There was silence.

"Are you done?"

"Yes," said Nora. She slid her hand up Abja's shirt

and twisted a nipple until it hardened. Abja pulled Nora's hand away.

"You know that's not what I meant."

"I do know that's not what you meant. Yes."

"Then explain how this sky could be an Arizona sky."

They were lying on their backs on the roof of Nora's hotel. Abja had put down a blanket. She seemed always prepared for the dirtiness. Nora was always surprised.

"Turquoise, red, orange," said Nora, pointing to the layers of the sky. "Do you understand the word *garish*?"

"Are you trying to teach me?"

"I would not presume to teach you anything," said Nora.

"Then maybe, yes, explain that to me too. The word *garish*."

"Not quite ugly. Tacky."

"Tacky?"

"Like garish."

"You are no teacher."

They were holding hands. Despite the heat of the city, of the roof itself, there was a breeze glancing the tops of their bodies that night.

"In Arizona, I grew eucalyptus. I swam almost every day. There was a pool in the backyard."

"I have been swimming four times in my life," said Abja.

"Including the day you were born."

"Yes," said Abja. "Including the day I was born. I like your memory."

They were quiet awhile. Abja squeezed Nora's hand and Nora squeezed back.

"I have three babies in Arizona," Nora said finally.

There was more silence.

"What do you think of that?"

"I think that I knew you had babies, but I did not know how many."

"How did you know?"

"Your breasts," said Abja. "You have the breasts of a mother."

A beetle brushed against Nora's thigh, she shook it away.

"They aren't babies anymore. But I can't imagine them as anything else. I'm stilted that way. I can only think of what is or what has been. I can't see anything else. There's no creativity up here." She knocked on her head with a fist.

"Do you want to tell me about the babies?"

Car horns now, children yelling and laughing from the streets below, cans being kicked. A caricature of a city, but the caricature came from somewhere. Mumbai spreading beneath them, people everywhere, it was too much for Nora even to think about, much less to try to imagine.

"No," she said at last. "I just wanted you to know."

"Look at me," said Abja. She did, and they kissed. "Now look again at the sky." Nora did as she was told, and Abja kissed her neck.

"There is something," said Nora.

"There is something?"

"I think I'm sick."

"Because of the drinking," said Abja. When she spoke, she spoke the words wetly, softly into Nora's neck. "This is something you know I agree with. I would not mind if the drinking were less."

"Yes," said Nora. "But no, that's not what I mean. I think I'm dying."

"Now, see, there is that imagination you think you do not have."

"No," said Nora. "Not imagination." She took Abja's hand and placed it on her left breast. Abja caressed it. "Here," said Nora, directing Abja's fingers. "Feel." Abja touched the lump, moved it back and forth between her fingers. "Do you feel it?"

Abja sat up. "What is that?" She was angry.

"Please lay back down. I don't like it down here without you."

Abja did as she was told, but she did not look at Nora. The orange was fading into the red. The turquoise was nearly black. The sky was almost any other night sky.

"What I think is cancer," said Nora finally. "It's in my family. Cancer all over. We're unlucky like that."

"Do not make this a joke," said Abja.

"This is not a joke." There were tears in the corners of Nora's eyes. "Not a joke at all. I can feel my body disappearing. Like it isn't always here. I can feel it. Do you believe me? Does that make sense?"

"It is time for you to go home maybe," said Abja.

"I like it out here. It's not too late yet," said Nora.

"That is not what I mean. You have gotten too good at misunderstanding me. I don't like it."

"You do like it," said Nora. "I'm sure of that."

"Then I do not like *you* very much right now."

"I'm sure of that too," said Nora.

"Listen, little American girl," Abja said, holding her hand again finally. There was sweetness in her voice again, almost something maternal. "I think it is time you go back to your family. I think it is time you go back from wherever you came. And I think those people who you have left behind, I think they will find you a good hospital and I think you will live to become an adult."

Nora cupped one of Abja's breasts in her hand. She moved her body so that she was speaking into the cupped breast, which, though covered, was moist with sweat.

"I'm not a child," said Nora. But she was a child. She would always be a child. How could she ever be anything more than a child to us?

"Yes, I remember you telling me that. And no, you are not a child. But do this for me, yes?"

"No," said Nora. "I like it here. This is where I want to be. For the first time, this is exactly where I want to be. Can you understand that? I like the noise. It will be a good place for me to die. You'll see. I'm going to be good at it. Just wait." Nora put a hand on Abja's face. "I'll make you very proud." Nora was full-out crying now, but she was also laughing, and the laughter, for the first time, frightened Abja. For the first time, she saw there was a very good chance that Nora truly was sick.

BUT, MORE LIKELY, WHAT ended up happening was this. Before Abja could help Nora die, before they could watch together as her body ate away at itself in a way very similar to how Mr. Lindell's own body must have eaten away at itself, Abja died in the bombings. Nora would have been there that day, just as Stu Zblowski and Marty Metcalfe swore she was, at one of the cafés. She was drinking beer. Abja was

HANNAH PITTARD

drinking milk and tea. A British tourist had asked to take their photograph. "Do you mind?" He motioned to his camera. Nora leaned into Abja, they locked their arms around one another. Their tattoos blurred together then, the designs becoming a seamless series of lines continuing from one woman's arm onto the other's. "Beautiful," he said, before moving away from them. "Beautiful."

The flattery of the photographer had put them both in a good mood. "I'll get you another beer if you ask me nicely," said Abja. There were days when they pretended the cancer didn't exist. When they behaved as if they'd never even discussed it.

"Kiss me," said Nora, and she did.

Abja was gone thirty, maybe forty seconds, when the first blast went off. It was loud—no—deafening. The sound came from all over, but the dust was across the street. The screaming was across the street. The next blast was closer, heavier. The dust was thicker, the screaming was more immediate. Nora turned to look inside, to see if she could still see Abja, but the café was gone. The people inside were gone. Or maybe it was a trick of the chaos. Maybe it was only the dust disguising the café.

There was more screaming, another blast. There might have been more after that, but she wouldn't remember. Nobody who was there would remember every blast. The stories were conflicting. Some would insist the first blast had come from Nora's café. Others would say that, no, the first blast had come from the café across the street from where Nora and Abja had been.

It took hours for the dust to settle, for the people to be hushed, calmed, treated. There was a bandage on Nora's arm when the news cameras started filming. She didn't know how the bandage got there. It's impossible to say whether or not Nora saw the news anchor from her—our—hometown. If she had seen her, she definitely would have recognized her. It's strange, either way, to think that Nora would linger there in the background. Shock, probably, nothing more than that. Though there is the chance it was deliberate, as small a cry for help as you can imagine. She'd thought, perhaps, something like this: *If they see it, if they find me, okay. If not, okay.* Or maybe not. Maybe there were no thoughts at all anymore. Maybe her brain had been reduced once again to images only, no words. A bottle of beer, a cup of tea, a hennaed arm, a camera, a British accent, a kiss, a scream, dust.

There is only that brief footage. We've all seen it by now, one by one, at work, our office doors closed behind us as if we were doing something dirty. We found the footage online, used our work computers to watch it over and over to confirm or contest what Marty Metcalfe and Stu Zblowski had seen.

The footage, honestly, isn't completely convincing. The image of the would-be Nora Lindell is tiny, blurry at best. The woman is red-haired. She is both full-figured and slight, just as Nora would have been by then. The face appears freckled, though perhaps it's merely sunburned or dirtied from the blasts. There is a bandage on her right arm and throughout the forty or fifty seconds of footage, she stands, rather dazed, her left hand spread open across her chest, which appears to be hennaed, though it might just be the soot and our eyes turning the randomness of filth into the intricacy of design.

What is convincing, though, is this: Both Marty and Stu, in two different living rooms, on two different television sets, in two different cities—Stu at the side of his newly pregnant wife on a soft leather sofa in New England, and Marty on the fabric love seat his grandmother had given him in a two-story Craftsman three streets over from the house where he grew up—both these men saw the image of this wounded redhead in Mumbai, and both believed it was Nora Lindell. All the more compelling that Marty would have noticed the figure at all since the news anchor, his lady love, should have been the only thing occupying his interest.

But for the cynics—for the nonbelievers, for those who require something more tactile and less spiritual

than a simple thought shared by two dissimilar men—
we offer this: the photograph. We have all seen it. It
was Winston Rutherford who saw it first, and without even meaning to. For the rest of us, it was less
accidental. We went where he told us to find it. The
southwest wing of the newly built media and news
museum in D.C. Enlarged, mounted, full color, the
photograph hangs amid the permanent collection of
the now-famous photographer Eli Brown.

The photograph is titled, simply, *Mumbai, Four
Minutes to the First Blast.* The women in the picture are
stunning, though it is true that the Westerner seems
sickly, skinnier than she ought to be. The Indian,
on the other hand, is something out of *National Geo-
graphic.* She is brown, with even browner tattoos that,
it's also true, appear to jump from the skin of her dark
arm onto the skin of the white and freckled Westerner's arm. Is it a tourist with her guide? Is it a teacher
and her student? Are the women a couple? Are they
lovers? Are they in love? These things are impossible
to tell. But yes, they have to be. Is it Nora Lindell?
Well, this, too, is impossible to tell.

But doesn't it have to be? Because haven't we all
made this decision, all come to this common conclu-
sion. All but Winston Rutherford, who will tell you,
quietly and respectfully, that the woman in the photograph is *not* Nora Lindell. He will tell you this and

Winston Rutherford's wife lost the first baby, and the second. It doesn't seem right to quantify lost babies, to say one was harder than the other to lose. But the first baby was its own brand of torture since she took it fully to term. They found out the week before the due date that the baby's heart had stopped, and the next day Maggie Rutherford was forced to deliver a stillborn baby. Imagine that. Because we do. We imagine it all the time and we hate ourselves when we feel relieved, grateful, that our own wives have never fallen victim to the same tragedy.

It's a relief that comes over us during solitary moments—brushing our teeth at night at the bathroom window, walking the dog alone in the morning fog—suddenly being indescribably thankful. The feeling fills our stomachs, wells up into our throats, and it's hard not to let out a laugh. It's hard not to want to let out a full-on yell, something primal and guttural, as if an untamed sound alone could describe the simple relief that we are here, that we are alive. Standing at the edge of the ocean, watching a sinking ship in a storm, we wipe our brow and wonder, in disbelief, at our own good fortune.

We went to the baby's funeral. The box was so small we couldn't tell if they'd had the body cremated after all. We felt guilty just wondering.

It wasn't our first funeral. Our first funeral was Danny Hatchet's mom's. We didn't know it then, of course, but our next funeral would be Mr. Lindell's. And after that, Minka Dinnerman's. Maggie's second baby never made it past the first term, and they didn't have a funeral.

You're not supposed to tell people you're pregnant. We learned that from our wives. You're not supposed to tell anybody until you're out of harm's way. Maggie and Winston told everyone when they were pregnant with that second baby. You should have seen them. They threw a party—a small one, but most of us were there. We checked with our mothers before going, confirming that the right thing to do was leave our own children at home in the care of babysitters

THE FATES WILL FIND THEIR WAY

or, better yet—*if there's nothing else going on, as long as we have you on the phone?*—in the care of their grandparents. Funny that we thought to not bring our kids even before we knew the party was to announce that second pregnancy.

Maggie glowed. She really did. She looked healthy in a bygone way. She looked healthy like we imagine our mothers must have looked when they were her age. Oh and when they told us, we were so happy for them. Winston Rutherford demanded we drink the good scotch in the kitchen while our wives talked in the living room and sipped Champagne. We didn't understand it at the time—the way, one at a time, our wives gave us these sad, puppy-dog eyes, as we walked into the kitchen—sad, like they were sorry we were so stupid all the time or like they were just sorry for people in general—but we understood later.

Unbuttoning our shirts, tossing away our trousers, the kids tucked into bed, we might have said something as careless and harmless as, "What'd I tell you? The Rutherfords are going to be just fine. Just fine." And it was that little remark, that daft utterance, that set our wives off, let loose their tongues. We were idiots. Maggie was only eight weeks, they said. Eight weeks! Didn't we understand? Well, yes, maybe, we understood. But, no, they told us, we didn't understand because Maggie might as well not even be pregnant, might as well not even be thinking of this thing in her uterus as anything real for at least another month. It was irresponsible, our wives told us, irresponsible for her to be getting her hopes up, Winston's hopes up, our hopes up. It was just plain irresponsible.

"But isn't it her right?" we asked gingerly, quietly. "Isn't it her right to get her hopes up? Maybe high hopes are what will keep the baby alive?"

This—our sheer stupidity, our genuinely naïve idiocy—is, more or less, where each of them broke down in tears and succumbed to our lousy, worthless hugs. What did we know? Nothing.

"Oh," they cried. "Oh, oh, it's not you. I'm not angry at you. I'm just so sad for her. So sorry. Oh, I hope it lives. I do. I do."

And we all hoped it lived. We hoped like hell that little thing took root and grew and grew and lived to be born and breathe. But it didn't. There was a third pregnancy, but no party and no baby.

NOT TOO LONG AFTER losing that third baby, Winston Rutherford told us about the photograph on the wall of the museum in D.C.

Winston had taken Maggie to D.C., presumably as a break from their lives, a break from babies. They stayed at one of those little historic hotels tucked into a cobblestone neighborhood—the kind of place our wives are always begging us to take them. They walked all over, ate out each night, just what our own wives would love. Winston took her to every museum, including the new media museum where he inadvertently happened upon the picture of what looked like Nora Lindell. He didn't show the photograph to Maggie. Somehow he thought it would make things worse. Like our mothers, our wives were troubled by our refusal to let Nora Lindell go. They thought, perhaps rightly, that it was an indulgence from which only jealousy and regret could come.

D.C. didn't go as Winston had hoped. It's not that Maggie cried or made scenes or that she was impossible to console. It's more that she didn't do much of anything. At dinner, she ate what was put in front of her, drank what was poured into her glass. He took her dancing one night and she moved like a zombie. "Like a fucking zombie," he said. "Like she might break if I squeezed too hard." She seemed younger than ever, Winston told us, but not in a good way, not in a youthful, carefree way. Instead, she seemed to be regressing mentally. He didn't know how else to say it. She was losing weight, losing sleep, and he didn't know how to talk to her anymore. "I'm losing her," he said. "I think I'm losing her."

One night, a week or two after getting back from

D.C., Winston woke up and Maggie wasn't in bed. He checked the clock; it was past four a.m. At first he thought she was in the bathroom and he almost fell back asleep.

He found her in the living room, the good scotch on the coffee table, a tumbler in her hand. It must have been going on for a while, possibly since the second baby. He left her on the sofa, went to the upstairs office, closed the door behind him, and called Chuck Goodhue, who woke up his wife, and asked what they should do. Both Peg and Chuck ultimately suggested counseling, preferably for both of them, definitely for Maggie. Funny to think that the Goodhues are probably the last people any of us would call now for marital advice. But, back then, it seemed reasonable. Names and phone numbers were exchanged. Recommendations were made. Maggie started seeing a therapist twice a week. They stopped trying to have babies.

TEN YEARS LATER, MAGGIE told Winston she was having an affair. "I can't sleep without the dog," was all he said when she told him.

"Classic," said Danny Hatchet when Winston told us the story. "Classic Rutherford. I love it. *I can't sleep without the dog.* Man, that must have pissed her off."

A few of us shook our heads, like we were disappointed in Danny's inability to see the bigger picture. We shook our heads and waited for Danny to produce one of his ubiquitous joints from thin air, but he didn't. Maybe we'd shaken our heads once too often, and for the first time, Danny was trying to be good. What we hadn't anticipated was how much this annoyed us. It seemed some of us had become accustomed to those unexpected pot breaks during tough times. Some of us had come to look forward to them. Danny must have sensed something amiss because, out of nowhere and in response to nothing, he said, suddenly, "I'm forty-three years old. We're forty-three years old. At some point we have to start acting like it."

If we'd been paying attention to anything other than ourselves, our wives, the Rutherfords, we might have been more curious about Danny's lack of weed at that moment. We might have been curious about any part of Danny's life for that matter, and how, in spite of being one of our oldest friends, he seemed to become less and less clear to us. There were so many mysteries. What, for instance, were those packages that were always in the backseat of the Nissan whenever we bothered to glance inside? We'd assumed they were drugs and so we never asked. But we now wonder if they weren't really care packages for Sissy and the girls. If we'd been more curious, we might have understood or at least guessed that Danny's sudden ambition to be drug free after three decades as a pothead had something to do with his real, if not completely ridiculous, desire to make a go of it with Sissy Lindell, though she lived six states away. Perhaps Nora had never been his preoccupation, in the way that she had been ours. Perhaps it was Sissy all along.

We really might have been able to put these things together, but we didn't. We were too busy with our own lives.

MAGGIE RUTHERFORD WAS THE one to move out of the house. She moved, in fact, out of the state, someplace south—Florida maybe?—with a man she'd met at a grieving seminar.

"You can't grieve forever," Winston yelled as she pulled out of the gravel drive on Sycamore for the last time, a new man in the driver's seat.

And as far as any of us know, Maggie Rutherford, née Frasier, finished out her life in Florida, grieving for three children she never even had, married to a man who had also devoted his life to sadness.

We never understood why Minka Dinnerman's dad kept a copy of *Hustler* tucked in the recess behind the base of the toilet in the first-floor bathroom of the Dinnerman house. Mrs. Dinnerman was the hottest of all the moms. In some ways, it was a shame that she had to be called a mom at all. It seemed beneath her station. Or, as she might have said, *a station beneath me.*

At any rate, we all thought it was kind of weird– Mr. Dinnerman's greedy and unappreciative need to have more than one hot naked lady in his life. Probably we thought it was also weird that Trey Stephens bothered to look behind the toilet, but before we could think too much about what Trey's poking around through other people's things might mean or lead to, he reminded us that there was a real live copy of *Hustler* magazine just waiting to be perused.

We started taking turns using the first-floor bathroom whenever we visited the Dinnerman house. Maybe Mrs. Dinnerman thought it was strange—four to eight boys stopping by on any given day, each of them needing to use the bathroom at some point during their visit—or maybe she knew what we were up to. She was definitely the kind of woman who knew more than she let on. She was, it occurs to us now, also the kind of woman who might have purchased a girlie mag and put it in a somewhat obvious hiding spot where her teenage daughter's male friends might "accidently" discover it. Who knows? Anything is possible. (In retrospect, we should have wondered that Trey never bothered using the Dinnerman bathroom once he'd made the rest of us aware of the magazine's existence. At the time, we suspected it was because he wanted extra time with Mrs. Dinnerman, despite his protestations that she didn't "do it for him.")

What's funny now is thinking about Minka Dinnerman—at the time more mousy than cute—sitting upstairs in her bedroom doing homework with a couple of her girlfriends while Chuck Goodhue, the man who would one day risk his marriage to be with her, was jerking off in her downstairs bathroom. Who could have predicted a thing like that?

And who could have predicted that their five-year affair would be discovered only because of a car crash (Minka's), and because of an unexpected display of emotion (Chuck's)? It was awful the way Peg Goodhue's cheeks went all scarlet when Chuck started crying at the funeral. Her whole body turned blotchy and pink. In general, Peg wasn't what you'd call the delicate type. Something about her psychiatry degree usually filled us with dread and suspicion, not sympathy and sorrow. But the day of Minka's funeral, she seemed like a little girl, all pink and red like that. It made you itch just to see her. Obviously, nothing was for certain the day of the funeral, but it would have taken an idiot—Danny Hatchet? Was it Danny who had to ask what all the fuss was about after the ceremony?—not to realize the implications of Chuck's tears.

IT'S EASY TO HATE Chuck for being so careless. It's not like he met Minka five years into a lackluster marriage. They were already sneaking around as early as that Christmas party with the chili lights and the oily hors d'oeuvres. It's easy to hold him accountable, to get mad at him. His infidelity did nothing for our own home lives. For at least a few weeks after the gossip broke, *Peg Goodhue v. Chuck Goodhue* became *Wives v. Husbands.* "They're trying to make it work," we told our wives whenever the subject came up. "You're more mad than she is."

"That's not the point," our wives said. "The point is men are idiots. Peg's gorgeous."

"Minka wasn't so bad-looking, either. Jesus, look at her mother."

"You're disgusting," they told us.

"Minka's *dead*," we said. "You can't be jealous of a dead woman." Maybe we said this last line with a little bit of a chuckle, maybe while we used a foot to shut the refrigerator door, while we twisted a cap off a cold bottle of beer.

"The affair still counts," they said, slamming the swinging door to the kitchen behind them, a futile but amusing effort to witness, the door swinging limply in their wake.

WHERE WE GREW UP, nobody went around saying that they weren't getting married, that they weren't going to fall in love, have children, raise a family. You didn't have to talk about it one way or the other; it was something we all assumed, especially the girls. That said, it's hard to pinpoint when it started being odd that so-and-so wasn't married, that they weren't even dating. But at some point, it *did* become odd.

Minka, for instance, we noticed wasn't married when our wives started suggesting she not be invited to holiday parties. "It's *strange*," they said. "Don't you think? That she doesn't even date? Maybe she's interested in one of you." Whenever they suggested something so outlandish, we couldn't help but laugh, make light of their worry. Because, truly, it had never even dawned on us—none of us but Chuck Goodhue—that Minka was game for something like an affair.

While we didn't really understand what Minka's singleness had to do with her right to attend our parties, we did understand that oddball requests from our wives, left ungranted, led to week-long silent treatments that ultimately ended in our caving anyway. It was a strange request, perhaps, but not one worth fighting over. Minka Dinnerman was definitely not worth fighting over.

Danny Hatchet and Trey Stephens' singleness stood out to us more. Maybe because they made it stand out, especially at bachelor parties or when poker games ran late and some of us had to leave before the game ended because our wives needed relief from watching the kids. "They're asleep," we argued, hoping to prolong the curfews they'd imposed. "What do you need relief from?"

"That's not the point," our wives would say when we complained. "That's why it takes *two* people to have a baby. If babies could be raised by one person, we'd be able to make them all on our own." We winced at how naturally they had developed what Danny Hatchet had, since Mrs. Hatchet's suicide, referred to as mom-logic.

It's difficult to remember whose idea it was–ours? our wives'?–to start setting Trey Stephens up with the single women we knew from work. (This was what? five? seven years before the incident involving Paul Epstein's daughter?) Maybe we were tired of Trey being single. Maybe we really thought he needed a companion. Yet we never even considered setting up Danny Hatchet with the single women we knew. Trey was more viable than Danny, more accessible, more normal. Trey had recently come into money, was essentially a man of leisure at the young age of thirty-five. Danny still wore sweatshirts, still lived paycheck to paycheck, still worked construction on and off as the mood struck him. Danny Hatchet rented; Trey Stephens owned. There was no question which of the two we'd be introducing to the single women from our law firms and doctors' offices.

Double dates with Trey were always fun. He drank well, ate well. His public school taste had somehow become more refined than ours. Maybe money was its own refiner. At any rate, his taste was inspiring. It made us want to appreciate wine. It made us happy to spend money. He was also able to charm our wives without coming across as a sleaze. For some reason–though they deny it now–Trey was one of the few friends they approved of. Maybe they liked flirting with him and we were the naïve ones. But honestly, they just seemed to enjoy his companionship, his enthusiasm for *their* company. Almost like he brought out the youthful forgotten girl inside them–asking them questions about crushes they'd had in high school, about former flames, about sneaking out of the house late at night, about their first prom. Who knows what it was? What we noticed, as their husbands, was that they were always a little more fun to go home with after a night out with Trey. Always a little more bubbly, flirty, a little bit tipsier than usual.

In some ways, Trey had matured more quickly than we had into a man who told the sorts of jokes our fathers used to tell and we'd roll our eyes as if to say *enough already*, but whatever girl we'd brought home to introduce him to would giggle. And so as much as we thought our fathers were total cornballs, we kind of liked that they could charm our girls for us.

How Trey developed this quality without children of his own, we didn't know. He might have learned it from his own father–Mr. Stephens was the type of guy who would get a little liquored up and come downstairs to the basement and start telling a story or giving a piece of advice that everyone but Trey thought was mesmerizing. There was that one party–maybe right after Danny Hatchet hit the dog?–when he came downstairs just as the last of us were about to leave and started telling us how to write country songs. He said, "What you've got to do, what you've got to do is, the next time you're a little bit drunk, you're a little bit high–" he winked in the direction of a cluster of girls "–you go outside, sit under the stars, maybe with a girl, definitely with a girl, and you write a country song. That's it. Get a little high. Get a little drunk. Write a country song. Make a million dollars. That's my advice, boys. Take it. Live it. Don't let there be a buffer between your heart and your mouth. Wisdom to live by. Take my word for it."

The only time Mr. Stephens became grating to the rest of us, and not just Trey, was when he was aware of his own charisma. Somebody–Drew Price? Paul Epstein? almost definitely someone short–would say something incidental, offhanded, like, "Oh, man, you've got to write that down. That's brilliant," and suddenly Mr. Stephens was off, a lunatic instead of a visionary: "That's right," he'd say, tumbler in hand. "A buffer. Ha! Don't let there be a buffer between your hands and your mouth. Your heart and your mouth. Whichever. You get the picture. Epstein, write down whatever it is I said the first time and remind me tomorrow. Probably a country song of its own. Write it down. You need a pen?" Suddenly Mr. Stephens had gone from a welcome interruption to a full-fledged intrusion; his interruption went from lasting five, ten minutes at most to sometimes lasting an hour.

If Trey had learned his charisma from his father, he'd learned to temper it with control and caution. "Too cautious," our wives say now, in retrospect. "There was always something too cautious about him. Like he was pretending. Like he was trying very hard to fit in." At the time, we swear they didn't see him that way. None of us did. We saw him as a fortunate, as a charmer, whose one shortcoming was that he hadn't found a woman worthy of his steady attention. But that was hardly Trey's deficiency, we thought. That was a limitation of the town, a limitation of the drab friends we had. We were to blame. Not Trey. Never Trey.

But then Ginger Epstein turned thirteen and Mrs. Epstein walked in on them. Our mothers called. "Can you imagine?" they said. "Can you even imagine?"

"No," we said, and we couldn't. We really couldn't even imagine.

AFTER MINKA'S FUNERAL, NOBODY thought the Goodhues would last. Nobody thought their marriage would survive. If the Rutherfords couldn't get through three dead babies, how could the Goodhues get through a five-year affair? But they did. Somehow. Something to do with Peg and that psychiatry degree and her stern Northern upbringing. Who knows? Peg wasn't one of us. She never had been. Chuck had met her in college, brought her back to our town to start a practice, raise a family. And, in spite of everything, they did just that. They stayed together, raised two of the prettiest girls in the neighborhood, and somehow seemed better off for the affair.

Mrs. Dinnerman, after the funeral, aged quickly. Overnight, she went from being an older woman you still had to consider sexually to being, well, old. Parents aren't supposed to lose children. Everyone knows that. Mr. Dinnerman sold his fleet of Mercedes, put the pink Greek Revival on the market—Jack Boyd and his second wife, Molly, snatched it up immediately—and the Dinnermans moved to Russia. And, like that, it was as if Minka and her mother had never even been here, had never even existed. The only thing they left behind—Jack showed us during

the housewarming party while our wives were check-
ing out the upstairs bedrooms, marveling at Molly's
renovations, trying hard to pretend not to mind that
she was only twenty-five, ten years their junior—was a
ratty copy of *Hustler*.

It was two counties over, so we didn't take notice when bones were found during the construction of a new high-rise on the bank of the river. *River Bank Condominiums.* The name was uninspired. *If you lived here, you'd be home now.* A stupid slogan, but they had a point. If we *did* live there, we *would* be home by now. The problem is that the investors hadn't done their research. They were banking on home-buyers who didn't exist. They were looking for early retirees who wanted a small town with a great view. But the amenities didn't exist two counties over, not yet. And so the building probably would have stopped eventually, regardless of the bones they found. The bones simply provided an excuse.

Marty Metcalfe's construction crew had been hired for the build-out. And if Marty hadn't been fired for public drunkenness (and his entire crew fired along with him), he would have been there on the Tuesday they discovered the bones and called the police, and we all might have heard about them sooner. We all might have been able to accept the real possibility of Nora, a Catalina, a stranger, and a struggle in the woods. Might have been able to. But Marty had been fired—he said he'd been laid off when they ran out of funding, but one article we *had* taken notice of in the local paper that year was in regard to a police report, a prostitute, and Marty's public intoxication—and so it took two years from the time the bones were found for us to finally hear about them.

WE WERE FORTY-FOUR, NINE years after Minka Dinnerman's funeral, when Gail Cummings, an over-ambitious journalist—who wasn't even from our home-town—did some research, put two and two together, and suggested to her editors that the bones, when they were tested, might belong to the missing Nora Lindell. The police were less impressed by Ms. Cummings' research skills than perhaps they should have been, but she pursued the connection on her own.

What's funny is that she came to us for contact information for the Lindells. "Do you know where

I can find Mr. or Mrs. Lindell?" she asked when our wives passed us the receiver, after she'd introduced herself and her purpose.

"The Lindells," we said. "The name sounds familiar. But no, no, I definitely don't know what happened to that family." Our wives shook their heads and left the room. We reasoned we were being protective. "A missing girl? It's been so long. Was that the Lindells?" What kind of journalist wouldn't have known Mr. and Mrs. Lindell were dead? We reasoned that if we were going to help someone, it wouldn't be someone so decidedly uninformed.

It was Danny Hatchet who refused to play along. In spite of the phone tree the rest of us had put into place in order to foil the journalist—Chuck Goodhue calling Winston Rutherford calling Stu Zblowski calling Marty Metcalfe calling Drew Price calling Danny Hatchet—Danny disregarded our request and agreed to talk to her.

"The Lindells, the parents, are dead," Danny told her. "And Sissy, Nora's sister, lives out West now."

"Tell me more," said Gail Cummings, and he did.

OF COURSE, WHAT WE didn't know—how could we?—was that Danny was the only one of us with any real information. Any one of us could have told her the parents were dead. Any one of us could have told her that Sissy Lindell was living out West with a gaggle of girls. Any one of us could have told her that Nora Lindell went missing when she was sixteen and that she looked best in her uniform with her jean jacket rolled up at the cuffs and her knee socks not quite evenly pulled up. Any one of us could have told the journalist these things. But Danny—Danny was the only one who could, and did, tell her where and how to find Sissy.

What he said was this: "Listen, I've got to ask Sissy first. I need to make sure it's okay I give you her number."

"You mean you're in direct contact with Sissy Lindell?"

"Not at the moment," said Danny. "But I'm capable of it. Give me your number. Either I'll call you back or she will."

"Thank you, Mr. Hatchet. Thank you, thank you."

SISSY MUST HAVE DRIVEN straight through the night to get back here, because within two days of Danny Hatchet's phone call with Gail Cummings, she was spotted by Jack Boyd's second wife at the coffee shop at the end of Sycamore.

Sissy wouldn't have recognized Jack's wife because they'd never been introduced, but Jack's wife recognized Sissy from the photographs and the stories she'd seen and heard. Molly Boyd wasn't due to pick up her kids from the sitter for another few hours and so rather than get her coffee to go that day, she sat down at the table next to Sissy Lindell, it turns out, sitting across from Gail Cummings, who was attempting, unsuccessfully, to interview Sissy.

"They were talking about DNA," Molly told us as she put away the groceries the following Sunday. Jack had concocted a brunch the following weekend in order to get us over to his house to learn what Molly had heard. "The police want a sample. Sissy doesn't want to give it. That's pretty much all they talked about. The journalist wanted a reason."

"But what else?" asked Jack. "There must have been more." He prodded her as a sort of show-and-tell. We didn't mind.

"She's not nearly as pretty as everyone says," said Molly.

"Who isn't?" we asked.

"That Sissy woman. She looks older than she should, you know? Wrinkly."

We winced, thankful our wives were in the next room.

"But what else did they talk about?" Jack said. "Stay on topic."

"I told you. The reporter wanted to know why Sissy wouldn't give them a DNA sample. I don't know whose. Sissy's? Her sister's? They want to test some bones."

"It's Danny's fault," said Drew Price. "He ruined everything."

"Where is Danny, anyway?"

"Business trip," said Jack.

"Business trip?" we asked. "Since when? What does that even mean? A business trip to buy weed?"

"Beats me," said Jack. "He said he was headed someplace warmer for the weekend. Didn't ask."

"Warmer?" Drew said. "Like Arizona?" We ignored him.

"I don't see what the big deal is," said Molly. "Who cares if the journalist talks to Sissy?"

"You don't get it," said Jack Boyd. "You just don't get it."

"Guess not," said Molly, backing out of the kitchen through the swinging door, balancing a platter of mimosas for our wives in the next room.

AND MOLLY BOYD DIDN'T get it; it's true. But we couldn't articulate why we didn't want Sissy Lindell talking to Gail Cummings or why it felt like a betrayal that Danny had put them in touch. We couldn't articulate the *why*; we just knew it felt like we were being stolen from. It felt like something that was ours alone, and always had been, was slowly slipping away and, with it, our sense of security. We had earned our fantasies about Nora Lindell; we had kept her legacy alive. Who was this Gail Cummings to think she could barge in out of nowhere?

"You know where they found the bones, right?" It was Marty Metcalfe talking. Since the whole Trey Stephens fiasco, our wives had been pretty staunch about the no-single-childless-people-allowed rule. But we were at Jack Boyd's house and Molly, being so much younger, was hardly a woman who put her foot down. There was also the hope that Marty might be able to provide some unprinted details about the site.

"The journalist told us," we said. "Next to the riverbank, where your awful high-rise was going up."

"Yeah, well, one of my guys got hired onto the new crew, and do you know that they found two sets of bones? Dog bones and human bones?"

"What's your point?"

"It's just that—" But Marty stopped talking. It's like he couldn't say it out loud. For once we had all been silenced. There was no right way to talk about Trey and Danny and that dead dog. There were no good phrases to describe that memory or the story they had once told us so long ago about driving a couple counties over and covering the thing with leaves. We looked at the ceiling. We looked at the floor. We looked at our watches. We waited for words to return.

"Holy shit," Winston Rutherford said finally, and we all breathed out a little, relieved that at least one of us had recovered his voice. Winston was still one year away from learning that Maggie Rutherford had made a cuckold out of him. "The Wilsons' dog. Holy shit."

We were quiet after that, contemplative. Of course, even if the bones did belong to the Wilsons' dog, this didn't mean anything or prove anything, nor did it have any bearing on whether the human bones belonged to Nora Lindell or whether or not Sissy would provide Gail Cummings with the necessary DNA. The bones meant nothing.

And yet.

And yet, after a very long time of us feeling nothing, those bones definitely felt like something.

Marty Metcalfe, of course, was the kid whose mom—the year her husband divorced her, our senior year of high school—made him steal his own dog back from his father's house. It's a strange story, involving Mrs. Metcalfe, one incredibly scared Marty, and a giant Saint Bernard.

The way we imagine it is this: Mrs. Metcalfe—prematurely silver-haired, tall, wiry-thin, angry as hell about Marty's dad and his tennis pro, Denise Comfort, only a few years older than Marty—drove one Saturday morning to her former home, parked across the street, left the car running, and ordered Marty to get the dog.

Marty never talked about it. It's not the sort of

thing—if it had happened to us and not to Marty—we'd have been anxious to share with the others. So we don't blame Marty for keeping the details to himself.

We heard bits and pieces from Mrs. Metcalfe herself, one of the counselors hired by the school after Nora went missing. Blame the divorce, blame anything you want, but Mrs. Metcalfe was probably unfit for counseling that year. More often than not, she'd get off topic and—we think in an effort to relate to us, we truly don't believe she was *trying* to be inappropriate—tell us stories about her ruined marriage or her strained relationship with her son, our friend, Marty.

It's not like she'd ever come right out and say, "Well, this one time, Marty and I were sitting in the car and . . ." It's more like, on occasion, she'd stop us mid-sentence, mid-thought about Nora Lindell and where she might be, and say something like, "Have you ever stolen a dog, Winston? Tell me that. Have you ever thought about stealing a dog?" Or, to Paul Epstein, she might say, "Tell me what you would do if your mom parked outside your dad's house and told you to break in. What would you do?" To which Paul Epstein might have said, "My mom's house *is* my dad's house?" Or, to Chuck Goodhue, as Chuck was exploring aloud the possibility of the man in the Catalina as described by Drew Price and Winston Rutherford, she might simply have asked, "What I

woman? Do you think I'd still have a shot at normalcy?"

"Mr. Goodhue," said Mrs. Metcalfe. "Is there something you want to tell me? Have you been compromised? Is there something I should know?"

"Whoops," he might say. "Time's up."

OVER THE COURSE OF our senior year, we all took a cue from Chuck and, here and there, during our time with Mrs. Metcalfe, began working into our conversation ostensibly hypothetical but actually exact details of Marty's tryst with the news anchor. Probably, by the time we graduated, she believed an entire class of boys had been molested by a single older woman, whose identity we'd sworn to keep secret.

CHUCK GOODHUE MIGHT HAVE been joking when he posed the question about a boy and an older woman and the potential for normalcy later in life; he might have been joking, but we can't help occasionally reflecting on that question now as adults, as men with wives and with vulnerable children of our own. Because isn't it possible that—though we thought of it then as a sexy story, as something to be jealous of—an older woman preying on a young boy is just as dangerous as an older man preying on a young girl? Why didn't we consider that at the time?

Instead, we were jealous when Marty told us the story about him and the news anchor on New Year's Eve. A few of us truly believed that if we'd attended the party, it might have been us in the closet with the anchor instead of Marty.

In the weeks following the incident, we developed a keen interest in local events and politics. Our mothers thought we were growing up; they thought an interest in local news was the first step to really broadening our horizons. They imagined that, in college, we'd read the newspaper, subscribe to all the right journals. This was an important first step, they thought, which is why they were so disappointed when, sometime around spring break, we abruptly lost our interest in the news in favor of football or tennis.

Of course, Marty never lost his interest. Where we grew tired of the fantasy—finally admitting that it hadn't happened to us and probably never would no matter how many times we tuned in to her show—Marty grew obsessive, unwilling or unable to believe it wouldn't happen again.

WHAT HAPPENED WAS THIS: Trish Bowles, an older cousin of Tommy and Franco Bowles, had been asked to attend the Metcalfes' annual New Year's Eve bash. She was a local up-and-comer, one of our town's forty-under-forty types. The Metcalfes were looking to expand their own horizons. They were looking to make new friends (of course, what Mrs. Metcalfe would understand by the end of the school year is that Mr. Metcalfe was not looking to expand his repertoire of friends so much as he was hoping to replace them entirely, starting first and foremost with his wife).

Trish Bowles was happy to attend; it was a chance to hobnob with the bigwigs. Likely she was already a little tipsy when she got there. Marty hadn't meant to still be at home when the adults-only party started, but when Trish mistook him for a guest and not the Metcalfes' son, he decided to stick around. It was fun to pretend, he said. He brought her glass after glass of Chablis. But at some point, he slipped up and referred to Mrs. Metcalfe as his mother. Trish was embarrassed. Her face turned crimson. She was afraid people had seen her flirting with a seventeen-year-old. She bowed out of the conversation, choosing instead to spend the rest of the night talking with Denise Comfort and her friends.

"So when did the make-out session happen?" Drew Price asked. "Sounds like there was a lot of talk and that's about it."

"I'm getting there," Marty said. This was in Trey Stephens' basement, the night after the Metcalfes' party. Marty had secured a bottle of Wild Turkey, and we were passing it around while he was talking. "There's a buildup. That's what women like, anyway. The buildup."

What happened is that Trish didn't stop drinking Chablis while she was talking to the tennis pro and by the time she was ready to go, she'd forgotten why she'd been avoiding Marty Metcalfe and, surprising even herself, when no one was looking, she pulled him into the coat closet, giggling, and put his hand in places it had never before been on a woman's body.

When it was over, when they could hear people filing down the stairs headed for the coat closet, Trish—even as Marty could still taste the sticky white wine on his tongue—said in a panicked whisper, "You can't tell anyone. Oh, oh. This won't happen again. Oh, I'm sorry. Oh, what have I done?"

OF COURSE HE TOLD us and, at the time, woozy with Wild Turkey, it seemed so decidedly unfair that she'd chosen Marty. We were the ones who should have learned so early what women wanted and how they wanted it. We deserved that knowledge, not Marty.

But what we wonder now sometimes, sitting at the pool, watching our girls take turns on the diving board, is whether or not we'd even have a family—

whether or not these girls doing backflips not twenty feet away from us would even exist—if we'd gone into a coat closet with Trish Bowles or some other older woman.

And it's at times like these when we cannot help but shudder at the things adults are capable of. Why didn't we know better then? And what things are happening already that our own children don't know better about now? We cannot help looking at those wiggly, giggling girls splashing about in the pool just in front of us, their skin tanning, bordering on burning, and wonder what's taking place in their lives—in their strange and alien brains—that they're already keeping from us. What, right now, is taking place that we should be stopping but that we can't even see?

Trey Stephens had a heart attack and died in prison. It was October, the year we all turned forty-five, and we held a very private ceremony for him at Danny Hatchet's apartment. We didn't tell our wives, and out of respect we didn't invite Paul Epstein. Who knows? Maybe the mere act of getting together in honor of a pedophile is an automatic disrespect towards the family, towards the victim. But Trey, before he did those things to Ginger Epstein, was one of us. We'd grown up with him, down the street from him. Not too long ago, he'd been a friend, and his parting merited our acknowledgment.

It's unclear how we ended up at Danny's place. Maybe because he didn't have a wife to object to the get-together, though it seems more likely that we would have gone to the recently divorced Winston Rutherford's house. It must have been that before any of us could suggest Winston's place, Danny offered his and we felt bad about saying no. The day was supposed to be about Trey Stephens, after all. We didn't have time to worry about things like cramped space and mildewed coffee tables.

In other ways, it made sense. Perhaps more than any of us, Danny had been closest to Trey. The public schooler and the poorest of the private schoolers—destined to be either the most obvious allies or the bitterest enemies. But it was October; we were depressed, feeling older than we'd ever felt, and we went to Danny's apartment because we could, because we needed to get out of the house, away from our families, away from our wives.

IT WAS THE FIRST time we can remember actually asking Danny to give us weed. There was fake wood paneling on the walls of his apartment. Someone pointed out there wasn't a mirror in the bathroom.

"How do you shave?" asked Drew Price.

"Sitting down," said Danny. Drew could be a total ass when he wanted to and everyone knew it, especially Danny.

"At any rate," said Chuck Goodhue, "the weed."

He held out his hand towards Danny as if Danny might just reach into his pocket and pull out a joint the way he'd done his whole life. But Danny just shook his head. "I'm sorry," he said. "I don't have any."

We didn't believe him.

Chuck said, "Seriously, quit dicking around. Produce the pot."

But Danny said, "No, man, for real. I don't have any."

"What the fuck," said Chuck. "Way to come through for the team. Especially today. Today of all days you're going to hold out. What the fuck."

We only stayed another half hour after that, drinking beers and watching a basketball game that none of us really cared about. Danny stood by the window, looking up at the parking lot behind his basement apartment. We didn't talk about Trey. What was there to say? Instead, we thought about our cholesterol, our hearts, our families. We thought about how little had happened in our lives, but how quickly the little that had happened had actually gone by. It was hard not to be angry with our bodies, with our aging. It was hard to believe that we'd actually gotten this far and not figured out a way to stop it, to pause life, to enjoy it. Hadn't our own fathers been counting on just that—on our ability to outlast what they couldn't?

We drank our beers and eventually someone–
Chuck probably?–gave the cue that it was time to get
out of there. Danny looked hurt when we said goodbye in the parking lot. Maybe it felt as final to him as
it did to us. We were feeling dramatic that day. Why
shouldn't we?

Jack Boyd said, "Look, you've got to understand,
Danny, there are children involved. We've got to get
home."

"Yeah," said Danny. "I understand."

He glanced at Winston Rutherford, like maybe he
would stay since there were no children, and since
Maggie had just left, but Winston said, without being
asked, "I'm meeting some guys from work. They do
drinks once a week to get out of the house. Maggie
said it would be good for me."

"Maggie's gone," said Chuck.

"Thanks for the reminder."

"I think Chuck means that maybe you shouldn't
be taking her advice." Danny kicked at the curb.

"Yeah, maybe."

We walked to our cars. Chuck slapped Danny on
the back. "Sorry I snapped," he said.

"It happens," said Danny.

"Shit happens," said Chuck, getting into his car.

Danny shut the door and gave the window a final
knock.

"Shit happens," Chuck said again from the other side of the glass. There was a shared laugh between the two of them that, from where we were sitting in our own cars, looked sad, forced. The clouds overhead threatened snow. They would threaten snow almost every day that winter, though they would ultimately produce only an inch, just after Christmas. What a disappointment that would be to all of us; no matter how old we got, Christmas was never really Christmas without the snow.

Danny waited outside as we left the parking lot. It was like watching our moms watch us drive away to college for the first time. Something deep down felt like crying.

THAT NIGHT–LYING AWAKE, watching our wives' shoulders rise up, sink down with their easy female breathing–we didn't think about Trey Stephens as, earlier in the day, we imagined we would upon getting into bed. We didn't think about the gray cement cell where his heart finally gave out, or about his ashes and how there was no one to claim them and how none of us had volunteered. We didn't even think about Ginger Epstein, and whether or not her parents had told her or if she already knew because she'd somehow been getting news about Trey on her own. Instead, somewhat surprisingly, we thought about Danny Hatchet.

We thought about his dark skin and how it had kept him looking young, even as we continued markedly to age. We thought about his body, so lanky in high school, now somehow muscular and substantial. Our own bodies were turning soft, difficult. At some point in the last decade, Danny Hatchet's face had cleared up. Why hadn't we noticed that before today? The scars on his forehead had faded. When had that happened? There was whole skin around his cuticles, which were normally blistered with hangnails and infections. Was it possible that Danny Hatchet looked healthy for the first time in his life? Suddenly the image of Danny in our rearview mirrors—pathetic as he might have seemed as we drove away—was the image of a full-fledged man. Danny Hatchet had grown up. When the fuck had that happened? And how?

REMEMBER THAT YEAR IN middle school when Danny came back after Christmas break and told us about the flea market his mom had given him, and somehow we knew not to make fun of him? And remember how angry we got when Maggie Frasier told him that what he meant to say was *ant farm*, not *flea market*? His face turned so red that we thought he might cry. And, really, for a moment, we thought Winston Rutherford might punch Maggie—his future bride, his future ex-wife—in the face.

Already, that early, even before his mom died, we had learned to feel sorry for Danny. Why was that? Maybe it wasn't fair. Our sympathy. Our coddling. There is a vanity, after all, in believing you are better than someone else, and wasn't our fierce protection of Danny just that? Maybe, at the end of the day, we had something to do with his protracted childhood, his inability to move forward, advance in life, marry, have children, form a family. Maybe. Or maybe we were being too hard on ourselves. Impossible to say. But we did, that night, as our wives turned to face us and coax us into sleep, perhaps make mental notes that we should call Danny more often. Invite him for a barbeque. Maybe even Thanksgiving. Yes, we thought, Thanksgiving. Not knowing, of course, that by Thanksgiving, Danny Hatchet would be gone.

Because what we couldn't know the day of Trey Stephens' informal memorial, driving away from Danny's apartment, watching him watch us in our rearview mirrors, feeling so sorry for him, for all of us, really—what we couldn't know then was that in less than two months from that day, he'd be packed up and moved to Arizona with Sissy Lindell and all three of those strange little girls. If we'd known that, if we'd known what he and Sissy were already plotting–a life together away from us–we might have understood that Danny wasn't sad about being left alone or left behind. He was sad for us. He was already saying goodbye and we didn't even know it.

This is how we thought it would end. We thought it would end with Danny Hatchet and Sissy Lindell alone in that dark little bar on High Street the year we all turned forty-five. Mr. Lindell had been dead for twelve years. Minka Dinnerman had been dead for ten. It was the year Maggie Rutherford drove to Florida with a grief counselor. The year Winston Rutherford told her it was fine if she went, but she couldn't take the dog. Trey Stephens died in prison that year, and Ginger Epstein turned eighteen and moved in with a forty-year-old two states away. We were embarrassed for the Epsteins, embarrassed for ourselves as men. It seemed like the year for endings, and so maybe that's why we imagined it would end for them as well—for Sissy and Danny. We were ready for it to be over.

Nora Lindell, even if she'd actually made it past that night in the woods with the man in the Catalina, was probably dead by now too. Nothing had come of the riverbank bones, except to confirm that several dog bones and only one as-yet untraceable human bone had been found. Sissy must never have relinquished the DNA to the police, and Gail Cummings must not have been crafty enough to come up with any on her own.

It seemed we had all finally stopped looking for her, asking about her. It was a sickness, a leftover from a youth too long protracted. Of course we still thought about her. Late at night, lying awake, especially in early autumn, when we could fall asleep for a few weeks with the bedroom windows open, the curtains pulled halfway, a breeze coming in, and the occasional stray dry leaf, we still allowed ourselves the vague and unfair comparisons between what our wives were and what she might have been. At least we were able to acknowledge the futility of the fantasies, even if we still couldn't control them.

But that's beside the point now. The point is, how we imagined it ending was with Danny and Sissy sitting side by side at that bar on High Street, facing the mirror behind the liquor bottles. Danny still smoked.

Sissy had quit. She was in town because of the continued Gail Cummings debacle. Or maybe something
else. The point is, she was in town again, and she'd
given Danny a call.

"Some days I almost don't even think of her," said
Sissy. "Most days I do. You'd think I'd miss my dad or
even my mom. But I don't. I mean, I do, but it's Nora
who's there, front and center. You know?"

"I know," Danny said. "I do."

We imagined it would be sweet for them at the
end. They weren't in love. They'd never even suspected they were. Maybe Danny. Maybe for a minute
he held out hope that the feeling was there, in either
one of them. But as much of a fuckup as Danny might
have been, he wasn't stupid. None of us was stupid.
We were just dreamers. Caught in the dream of the
Lindells and what might have been.

"I brought you something." This we imagined
Danny saying towards the end of the night, when he
knew the goodbyes were imminent.

"It's not jewelry, is it?"

He laughed. "No, it's not jewelry."

"I can't smoke pot anymore. My lungs can't han-
dle it."

He laughed again. "Good guess, but no."

He reached into his back pocket and pulled out
his wallet. Sandwiched between the billfold was a

folded-up piece of paper. He put the wallet back in his pocket and slid the paper across the counter to Sissy.

"I can't tell if this is creepy or not," he said. He was looking at the mirror, not at Sissy. He was looking at himself, looking at what he'd become, what age had turned him into. When he spoke again, he spoke as much to his reflection as to Sissy. "I feel like maybe that's been the problem most of my life. Like I'm always doing things that might be creepy or might not be creepy, but I never mean them to be. You know?"

Sissy wasn't looking at Danny. She wasn't even looking at the mirror. She was looking down at the bar, at the piece of paper Danny had passed her.

"I took it from the telephone pole outside our house," he said. "I thought we could be friends back then. You and me. I thought maybe we'd have something to talk about."

We imagined little tears forming at the edges of Sissy's eyes. We imagined Danny wanting to touch her, wanting so badly to reach out and touch just the top of her hand or maybe even the small of her back, but he didn't.

"This picture makes her look like she's thirty years old," said Sissy. "She looks older than I did at thirty and she's only sixteen." She slid the missing sign towards Danny. "See? Look."

And they both looked down, genuinely trying to

see the thirty-year-old in the sixteen-year-old's face, trying to see the future, to see what might have been.

"Are you okay?" asked Danny.

"What do you mean? Am I sad? Yes. But will I wake up tomorrow? Yes."

"That's not what I mean." He nodded in the direction of her chest. She turned towards the mirror behind the liquor bottles. Her hand was on her sweater, clutching—the place where her heart must be.

"I'm fine," she said at last. "My heart hurts." She shrugged and moved her hand away. Danny said nothing. "My girls trick-or-treat on Halloween. Is that stupid? Is that normal? I don't know. Should it be a day of reverence?" Again, Danny said nothing. "Listen," said Sissy. "Is there anything else you want to ask me? About anything? I don't mind. About the girls maybe?"

"Everyone thinks she's my daughter," Danny said at last. "You know that, right? The littlest one."

"What do you think?"

"I think I'm not father material," he said. "I know that. That's one thing I know for sure."

"Do you want to ask me?"

"No," he said. "I really don't. Not unless you think I should."

She was quiet for a bit.

"No," she said. "I don't think you need to ask me."

"Okay," he said. "Okay."

They finished their drinks and Sissy asked the bartender for the check. Danny put his hand out to take it. "Please, Sissy," he said. "At least let me take care of this."

He looked down at the bar like he was embarrassed or like he might cry, or both.

Sissy, always somehow so young, so demure, so well-put-together, slid off her bar stool, kissed Danny's cheek, and said, "Anything you want." Then she walked out of the bar and out of his life forever.

Except.

Except that's not what happened. That's only what we wanted to happen. Why did we want it to end that way? Simple: because it's all that we could imagine.

IN THE END, THERE was no sad farewell, no protracted crying spell at the bar on High Street. There was nothing maudlin or tragic between them, no final few words about Nora and what might have been. Instead, there was Sissy—Sissy in real life—driving up to the back of Danny Hatchet's apartment in a new luxury SUV, packing up the last of his belongings just a few days after Halloween.

Chuck Goodhue's daughters saw the whole thing. They were walking home from school, slinging their book bags, occasionally trying to catch a stray leaf, when they saw the redhead get out of the car and walk down the stairs to Danny Hatchet's basement apartment.

They waited, not because they're nosey, but because there was nothing better to do. Maybe they thought they would see a fight, a scene, something ugly or maybe just something to gossip about. Who knows? But what they saw was Sissy coming back up the steps only a few seconds later, carrying a box, laughing, turning around to look at Danny, also coming up the steps, only he was carrying three boxes and his face was obscured, but Chuck Goodhue's girls say they were mostly just struck by Sissy's laughter, her mouth open wide, laughing like it was the best feeling on earth, laughing like there was nothing else to do but that.

Of course, at first, we didn't want to believe the Goodhue girls—they're not bad kids or anything, and they don't have a reputation as liars—but because it didn't fit with what we thought we knew about Sissy or about Danny. I mean, Danny was one of us. Born and raised. We saw him almost every day of our lives. It's one thing that we mistook Sissy's intentions, her aspirations, her dreams in life—Sissy's been a mystery since she left for boarding school. But Danny. We were unprepared for the discovery that Danny had been plotting a whole life separate from ours.

We called our mothers. We started to tell them what the Goodhue girls claimed to have seen, but they already knew. Paul's mom, Mrs. Epstein, had witnessed the whole thing as well, from the beauty parlor next to the apartment building.

"What a lovely lady," Mrs. Epstein had told our mothers, referring to Sissy Lindell. "Such a fine-looking woman, and she keeps her car very clean."

"Can you imagine?" we asked our mothers. "Danny Hatchet and Sissy Lindell? Can you even imagine it?"

"No," they said in a huff, a sudden change in their tone. "But it's really none of our business, is it?"

At the end of the day, we find ourselves somewhat unprepared, standing for a final moment at our bedroom windows, for the obvious realization that this—*this*, all around us—is our life.

It's that pink time of night. It's that time of night just before our wives come to bed. We can hear them rummaging about in the kitchen beneath us, turning off lights, returning a stray dish to its rightful place in the cabinet, giving the dog a final treat. They've just hung up the phone; just finished saying good night to whatever daughter or son has most recently gone off to college; just finalized holiday travel plans, having decided that flying really is a much safer option for a teenager than driving (because, honestly, it doesn't seem right that an eighteen-year-old, much less a sixteen-year-old, should even be allowed behind the wheel of a car)—but for that moment, as our wives climb the stairs, just before we hear their hands on the bedroom doorknob, we stand and look at the already darkening neighborhood spreading out beyond us, beneath us. The sky has turned from pink to purple, and where the streetlights flicker to life, the air is lavender, effervescent.

At the end of the day, it gets no simpler, no less complicated than to admit that this is our life. This is our home. Here is the window and the curtain and the first leaf of fall. This is our bedroom, and there is our pillow and there, just next to it, is our wife's pillow. On the other side of the bedroom door is our wife, about to come in, about to join us and swap her day clothes for pajamas. While we hang our ties and jackets, she will pull back the comforter, pull down the sheets. She will turn on both bedside lights and she will climb into bed, waiting.

Tonight we will sleep, perhaps holding one another, perhaps not, hoping somehow even as we sleep that there will be no telephone call in the middle of the night; hoping, simply, to wake up, to go about our day, to cover the pool finally tomorrow and admit the end of summer.

And, suddenly, something new is now certain,

something that we hadn't ever thought of before. There will come a day when we will think of Nora Lindell for the last time. We will think of her as the sixteen-year-old we once knew. We will imagine her in her field hockey sweats or in her uniform with her knee socks at half mast or maybe we will think of her in her jean jacket, with her back against the base of Trey Stephens' aquarium, braiding Sissy's hair. Whatever the memory, we will think of her, wonder what might have been, and we won't even know it while it's happening, but it will be the last time we ever think of her. That day will come. It is a certainty now. And it gets no more obvious than this: this—*this*, all around us—is our life.

ACKNOWLEDGMENTS

Thanks to everyone at Sterling Lord, especially Jim Rutman and Addie Wainwright. Thanks also to everyone at Ecco (Dan Halpern, Abigail Holstein, Allison Saltzman, etc.) but most especially to Lee Boudreaux, the world's gentlest and most acute editor.

I owe my family everything, but there are some specifics: I have to thank my mother, Stacy Stinchfield, who gave me her farm for the summer (and, yes, a little longer) in order to write more freely. If I hadn't had Lone Duck, I probably wouldn't have *The Fates*. I also have to thank my siblings, Noah and Greta, for their loyalty and support. Thanks also to the rest of my family–Jack Pittard, Lee Stinchfield, Brooke Galardi, Olivia and Georgia Pittard–for existing in the first place. This world would be unmanageable without you.

There are others to thank: Ann Beattie, for one. I could make a career of thanking Ann Beattie–for creating opportunities, for providing me encouragement, but mostly for not being afraid to expect more, to demand better. I also have to thank the University of Virginia and its other amazing faculty: Deborah Eisenberg, Chris Tilghman, John Casey. These people are such careful and caring teachers, and I am ever grateful for their attention and advice.

There are still others: Mundo Otal for lending me his perfect name, Emma Rathbone, Tom Bouman, Eve-Lyn Hinckley, Hugh Merwin, Zoe Pagnamenta, Benjamin Warner, Jim Shepard, Peter Fallon, everyone at *McSweeney's*, everyone at The Downtown Grille in Charlottesville, especially Robert Sawrey.

And Andrew, I of course have to thank Andrew Ewell, for sitting across from me while I wrote it all down, for distracting me when I needed to be–Frisbee, Pimm's Cups, Scrabble–and even when I didn't need to be–Frisbee, Pimm's Cups, Scrabble.

And, finally, to end where it begins, a quiet–if difficult–thanks to Malcolm Hugh Ringel, a.k.a. Pops, who was–and is–responsible for so much of who and how I am. My family only might recognize the similarities between the fictional obituary for Herbert Lindell and the very real obituary we wrote in 2006 for Malcolm Ringel. Still, it merits explanation: it would have been easy enough to create a wholly original obituary, but there was the strong desire to pay tribute, to keep the obituary somehow permanent, not ephemeral, and therefore preserve the memory, the man. And so, though there is no connection between the real Malcolm Ringel and the fictitious Herbert Lindell—except, perhaps, that they are both loved fiercely by their daughters—I could not help but indulge in the obituary's inclusion. And so, to my family, I say thank you for understanding. And to Malcolm, I say again (and again and again and again) you are missed, ever, ever missed.

JOHANNA SKIBSRUD

The Sentimentalists

Winner of the Scotiabank Giller Prize

Haunted by the horrific events he witnessed during the Vietnam War, Napoleon Haskell is exhausted from years spent battling his memories. As his health ultimately declines, his two daughters move him from his trailer in North Dakota to Casablanca, Ontario, to live with the father of a friend who was killed in action. It is to Casablanca, on the shores of a man-made lake beneath which lie the remains of the former town, that Napoleon's youngest daughter also retreats when her own life comes unhinged. Living with the two old men, she finds her father in the twilight of his life and rapidly slipping into senility. With love and insatiable curiosity, she devotes herself to learning the truth about him; and through the fog, Napoleon's past begins to emerge.

'Deeply moving ... I was engrossed by the elegant plotting and intelligent writing ... I was, simply, moved to tears.'
PATRICK NESS, GUARDIAN

'Remarkable ...Will stay with you long after you read the last page.'
CLAIRE MESSUD

'Beautiful ... subtle, sharp and truthful.'
THE TIMES

'Outstanding ...The emotional power is relentless ... an intelligent, reserved novel.'
IRISH TIMES

LAUREN GROFF

The Monsters of Templeton

Shortlisted for the Orange Broadband Award
for New Writers 2008

'The Monsters of Templeton *is everything a reader might have
expected from this gifted writer and more*'
STEPHEN KING

'*A vibrant patchwork of fact, fiction and myth . . . Beautifully rendered*'
DAILY MAIL

Willie Cooper arrives on the doorstep of her ancestral home
in Templeton, New York in the wake of a disastrous affair
with her much older, married archaeology professor. That
same day, the discovery of a prehistoric monster in the lake
brings a media frenzy to the quiet, picture-perfect town her
ancestors founded. Smarting from a broken heart, Willie then
learns that the story her mother had always told her about her
father has all been a lie. He wasn't the one-night stand Vi had
led her to imagine, but someone else entirely.

As Willie puts her archaeological skills to work digging for
the truth about her lineage, a chorus of voices from the town's
past rise up around her to tell their sides of the story. Dark
secrets come to light, past and present blur, old mysteries are
finally put to rest, and the surprising truth about more than
one monster is revealed.

'*A pleasurably surreal cross between* The Stone Diaries *and*
Kind Hearts and Coronets'
GUARDIAN